"There's no way to ge Jake asked.

Nog turned to Lek. "Do the Cardassians have a subspace radio?"

"Too late you are," Lek informed him. "Scavenged it already is."

Nog sighed. "Why did I know you were gonna say that?"

"Wait a minute," Jake said. An idea was starting to form in his mind. "I think you're on to something here. We don't have any equipment left, but the Cardassians do."

Lek shook his head. "Taken it all is. Tricorders, radio, everything we took."

"Not *everything*," Jake replied with a grin. "They still have a working spaceship."

His friends stared at him as if he were crazy. T'Ara's eyebrows rose so high they disappeared in her bangs. "Are you suggesting . . . ?"

"Yeah," Jake chuckled. "Let's steal their entire ship!"

Available from MINSTREL Books

For orders other than by individual consumers, Minstrel Books grants a discount on the purchase of **10 or more** copies of single titles for special markets or premium use. For further details, please write to the Vice-President of Special Markets, Pocket Books, 1230 Avenue of the Americas, New York, NY 10020.

For information on how individual consumers can place orders, please write to Mail Order Department, Paramount Publishing, 200 Old Tappan Road, Old Tappan, NJ 07675.

FIELD TRIP

JOHN PEEL

Interior illustrations by
Todd Cameron Hamilton

A
MINSTREL®
BOOK

PUBLISHED BY POCKET BOOKS

New York   London   Toronto   Sydney   Tokyo   Singapore

This book is a work of fiction. Names, characters, places and incidents are products of the author's imagination or are used fictitiously. Any resemblance to actual events or locales or persons, living or dead, is entirely coincidental.

A MINSTREL PAPERBACK *Original*

A Minstrel Book published by
POCKET BOOKS, a division of Simon & Schuster Inc
1230 Avenue of the Americas, New York, NY 10020

STAR TREK is a Registered Trademark of Paramount Pictures.

This book is published by Pocket Books, a division of Simon & Schuster Inc., under exclusive license from Paramount Pictures.

ISBN: 0-671-88287-2

First Minstrel Books printing August 1995

10 9 8 7 6 5 4 3 2

A MINSTREL BOOK and colophon are registered trademarks of Simon & Schuster Inc.

Cover art by Alan Gutierrez

Printed in the U.S.A.

This is for Bob and Patti McLaughlin,
with thanks for their hospitality

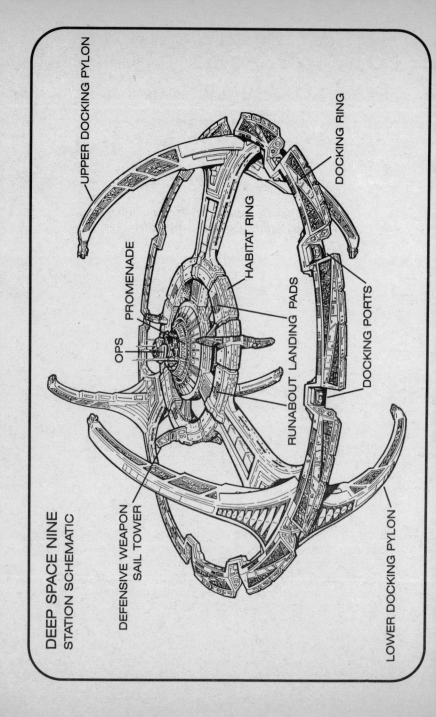

DEEP SPACE NINE
STATION SCHEMATIC

UPPER DOCKING PYLON

DOCKING RING

HABITAT RING

PROMENADE

OPS

DOCKING PORTS

RUNABOUT LANDING PADS

DEFENSIVE WEAPON
SAIL TOWER

LOWER DOCKING PYLON

STAR TREK®: DEEP SPACE NINE™
Cast of Characters

JAKE SISKO—Jake is a young teenager and the only human boy permanently on board Deep Space Nine. Jake's mother died when he was very young. He came to the space station with his father but found very few kids his own age. He doesn't remember life on Earth, but he loves baseball and candy bars, and he hates homework. His father doesn't approve of his friendship with Nog.

NOG—He is a Ferengi boy whose primary goal in life—like all Ferengi—is to make money. His father, Rom, is frequently away on business, which is fine with Nog. His uncle, Quark, keeps an eye on him. Nog thinks humans are odd with their notions of trust and favors and friendship. He doesn't always understand Jake, but since his father forbids him to hang out with the human boy, Nog and Jake are best friends. Nog loves to play tricks on people, but he tries to avoid Odo whenever possible.

COMMANDER BENJAMIN SISKO—Jake's father has been appointed by Starfleet Command to oversee the operations of the space station and act as a liaison between the Federation and Bajor. His wife was killed in a Borg attack, and he is raising Jake by himself. He is a very busy man who always tries to make time for his son.

ODO—The security officer was found by Bajoran scientists years ago, but Odo has no idea where he originally came from. He is a shape-shifter, and thus can assume any shape for a period of time. He normally maintains a vaguely human appearance but every sixteen hours he must revert to his natural liquid state. He has no patience for lawbreakers and less for Ferengi.

MAJOR KIRA NERYS—Kira was a freedom fighter in the Bajoran underground during the Cardassian occupation of Bajor. She now represents Bajoran interests aboard the station and is Sisko's first officer. Her temper is legendary.

LIEUTENANT JADZIA DAX—An old friend of Commander Sisko's, the science officer Dax is actually two joined entities known as the Trill. There is a separate consciousness—a symbiont—in the young female host's body. Sisko knew the symbiont Dax in a previous host, which was a "he."

DR. JULIAN BASHIR—Eager for adventure, Doctor Bashir graduated at the top of his class and requested a deep-space posting. His enthusiasm sometimes gets him into trouble.

MILES O'BRIEN—Formerly the Transporter Chief aboard the *U.S.S. Enterprise,* O'Brien is now Chief of Operations on Deep Space Nine.

KEIKO O'BRIEN—Keiko was a botanist on the *Enterprise,* but she moved to the station with her husband and her young daughter, Molly. Since there is little use for her botany skills on the station, she is the teacher for all of the permanent and traveling students.

QUARK—Nog's uncle and a Ferengi businessman by trade, Quark runs his own combination restaurant/casino/holosuite venue on the Promenade, the central meeting place for much of the activity on the station. Quark has his hand in every deal on board and usually manages to stay just one step ahead of the law—usually in the shape of Odo.

Historian's note: The events of this series take place during the first and second seasons of the *Deep Space Nine* television show.

FIELD TRIP

CHAPTER 1

It's perfectly safe; what could go wrong?"

Those words would come back to haunt Jake Sisko, but when he heard them spoken, he believed in them implicitly. It was only later that Keiko O'Brien's comment would be proved completely, utterly, and almost fatally wrong. . . .

Ms. O'Brien was conducting a lesson in astronomy for her small class of students. The computer projected a huge hologram of the Galaxy in the air just above their heads. The four quadrants of the Galaxy were lightly shaded, and Ms. O'Brien was using a laser pencil to point out the various stars.

"This is Sol," she explained, her beam of light picking out a small star near the edge of an arm of the Galaxy. "Earth is Sol Three. And this is what humans call 40 Eridani." She indicated a star close to the first. "That's the home star of the planet Vulcan. Both, as you can see, are in the Alpha Quadrant. Now, who can point out where Deep Space Nine is located?"

Naturally, T'Ara's hand was the first up. Jake was a much slower second. Jake's best friend, Nog, simply rolled his eyes in disgust.

Like most Vulcans, T'Ara was tall, slim, and very serious. She had long dark hair that was usually worn in a ponytail that freed her pointed ears and cut straight along her forehead, showing her slanted eyebrows. The Vulcan people didn't believe in allowing their emotions to rule their lives, and carefully kept their emotions hidden. Despite her maturity, T'Ara was only seven years old, and as a result her control over her emotions sometimes slipped. She was always ashamed when this happened, so her friends tried to pretend not to notice. Ms. O'Brien handed T'Ara the pointer, and she used it to illuminate a star in the Alpha Quadrant.

"Quite right," the teacher agreed. "Most of the worlds that we have explored lie within either the Alpha or Beta Quadrant. And, of course, we've started to explore some of the stars in the Gamma Quadrant thanks to the Wormhole."

What made Deep Space Nine so important had been the discovery of the Wormhole. This was a strange, almost unimaginable, tunnel through space. One end of it rested here, in space close to the planet Bajor. The other end of it was in the Gamma Quadrant, about 70,000 light-years away. Going through the Wormhole was a shortcut in space that saved ships years and years of travel. Before the Wormhole had been discovered,

nobody had known much at all about the Gamma Quadrant. Now there was a thriving trade, with traffic constantly passing back and forth through the Wormhole. The trouble was (from Jake's point of view) that he had never been allowed to go through it.

Jake shifted in his chair. "Only we never get to see those stars, do we?"

Ashley nodded. "That's right, Ms. O'Brien. We're sitting right on top of the Wormhole, but we've never been allowed even to peek inside it. It's not fair, is it?" Ashley Fontana was T'Ara's best friend, a human girl whose mother was one of Chief O'Brien's technicians. Ashley was slightly younger than Jake, with long blond hair and an ability to repair machines that was almost as good as she thought it was.

"Well," their teacher said carefully, "I'm certain it's just that everyone wants to make sure it's safe first."

"Oh, sure," agreed Jake. "They've been exploring the Wormhole for well over a year now. When do you think they'll consider it safe?"

T'Ara almost smiled. "Have *you* ever been through the Wormhole?" she asked Ms. O'Brien.

Their teacher was taken by surprise by that question. "Well, no," she admitted. "I haven't."

"Would you not like to go?" asked T'Ara innocently. Jake could barely stop himself from laughing. He could see the edges of the young Vulcan girl's lips twitching. She was really stirring things up!

"Well, yes," Ms. O'Brien replied. "Of course I'd like to go. But it isn't as simple as that and—" She broke off as she realized that all her students were looking at her with grins on their faces—except for T'Ara, who somehow managed to keep her amusement down to minor twitches of her lips. "That's quite enough of that," the teacher said firmly. "Let's get back to the lesson, shall we, and not get sidetracked?"

The lesson continued, and Jake thought he'd heard the end of the subject. To his surprise, he was wrong. That evening, as he and his father sat in their small apartment eating dinner, the computer by the door chimed.

Commander Sisko called out: "Come in!" The computer then opened the door.

Ms. O'Brien walked in. As she saw the almost-empty dessert plates, she said apologetically: "Oh, I'm sorry. I can come back later."

"That's all right," Jake's father said. "We've just finished. Jake, perhaps you could run the dishes to the recycler?"

Jake got the hint immediately; this was probably going to be adult business, and his father wanted him out of the way. "Uh, sure," he agreed. He was used to the procedure.

"No," said Ms. O'Brien, quickly. "There's no need for Jake to leave. In fact, he's part of the reason I've come here."

Commander Sisko shot his son a *what-have-you-done-now?* look. "I see. Has he been up to some mischief with Nog again?"

"No, nothing like that," the teacher assured him. "Quite the opposite, in fact. He and his friends made a suggestion in class today that seems to me to have some merit to it."

"Really?" asked Jake, amazed at the news. He hadn't expected her to complain about him, but one could never quite tell what went on in teachers' minds.

"Really," she agreed, smiling at him. To his father, she explained: "They raised the idea of a field trip."

Commander Sisko raised one eyebrow thoughtfully. "A field trip?" he asked.

"Yes," Ms. O'Brien replied. "None of them have really been off the station since we all came here, except for a few trips down to Bajor." Jake winced at that, remembering his last trip down to the planet with Nog, and the unexpected consequences of their impetuous decision. Ms. O'Brien continued: "They're all getting kind of restless, and I thought a field trip would do them good—get them off the station and into something a little more stimulating."

"I see," Jake's father said carefully. "So you want my permission, is that it? And, I assume, the loan of a runabout?"

"Exactly, Commander," agreed the teacher.

His father nodded. "Well, it sounds reasonable enough to me." He gave Jake a quick smile. "Travel broadens the mind, as they say, and these young minds need all the broadening that they can get. So, where do you intend to take them? The Fire Falls of Ushara? The Monastery Fortress of Kai-tona? The Gardens of Pure Delight?"

Ms. O'Brien shook her head. "None of those," she

admitted. "In fact, I wasn't thinking of anywhere on Bajor at all."

Commander Sisko shrugged. "Andros, then?" he asked, naming the next closest planet. "Or the Asteroid Belt?"

"Actually, I was thinking of Cetus Beta," Mrs. O'Brien told him.

It took a second for the name to sink in, and then Jake's father stared at her in astonishment. "Cetus Beta?" he repeated. "In the *Gamma Quadrant?* Surely you must realize that's completely out of the question?"

Jake had been following the conversation with interest —and then excitement—when his teacher had suggested a flight to a world in the Gamma Quadrant. His heart sank, though, at the firmness in his father's reply. "Aw, Dad!" he protested.

Commander Sisko frowned. "Don't 'aw, Dad' me," he said. To Ms. O'Brien he added: "Surely you realize how dangerous a trip like that would be, Keiko?"

To Jake's surprise, Ms. O'Brien didn't back down. "Not at all," she replied calmly. "I've done my home-work on this, Commander. Cetus Beta is in one of the closest planetary systems on the far side of the Worm-hole. There's no intelligent native species in the whole system, and absolutely no animal life of any kind on Cetus Beta itself. The entire world is completely popu-lated by plants. It's just about the safest planet we've ever discovered, and it's been checked out by two Federation science vessels and declared absolutely harmless."

Commander Sisko's frown softened a little. "I see. Anything else?"

"Just one more thing," the teacher answered. "My students are all getting restless, being so close to the Wormhole. Do you realize that they're all dying to see what it's like? And it's out there, luring them on. You know what children can be like, Commander. How long do you think it'll be before one of them decides to stow away on a ship heading out there?"

His father gave Jake a frown. "Knowing these rascals," he admitted, "I'm somewhat amazed that one of them hasn't tried it yet. So you are suggesting that an authorized trip through the Wormhole might serve to satisfy their curiosity?"

"An authorized, safe, and responsible trip," explained Ms. O'Brien. She seemed to be sensing victory. "Just ten of the students," she added. "Jake, Nog, T'Ara, Ashley, and six of the Bajorans. I'd go along, and there would be the pilot of the runabout, too. We could camp out on Cetus Beta for a week, then return. It's perfectly safe; what could go wrong?"

CHAPTER 2

Jake was having a great deal of trouble keeping his mouth shut. He was dying to jump in and try and help persuade his father. He knew, though, that he was likely to make his father more obstinate if he interrupted, so he managed somehow to stay quiet. He couldn't prevent the eagerness he felt from showing on his face, though, and his father saw it.

With a laugh Commander Sisko shook his head. "It looks as if I'd better agree," he conceded. 'If I don't, I'll have to have every ship leaving the station from now on searched to make certain my son isn't part of the cargo."

"Yes!" Jake exploded happily. "Way to go, Dad!"

"But," his father said, holding up a hand in warning, "it had better be firmly understood that you and the rest of your friends are to do *everything* that Ms. O'Brien says, or you'll all be grounded for the rest of your lives. Is that clear?"

"Yeah, you bet, absolutely," agreed Jake happily.

Turning to Ms. O'Brien, his father added: "All right, Keiko. I think you're correct. These youngsters have been cooped up on DS9 for too long. And Cetus Beta is probably a lot safer for them than even Bajor would be. You can have a runabout and a pilot for a week's stay. Let me check out the list of supplies you'll be taking and your schedule." He glanced at Jake again and grinned. "I hope you're planning on taking this trip pretty soon. I don't think your students will be able to contain themselves too long."

Ms. O'Brien gave a dazzling smile. "I was hoping we could go in a few days."

"Fine." Jake's father smiled. "Cetus Beta is a world full of plants, you say? Your own love of botany wouldn't have anything to do with that, would it?"

"A good deal," admitted the teacher. She had been the botanist on the *U.S.S. Enterprise* before she and her husband had been posted to Deep Space Nine. "But I chose it primarily because it's absolutely safe. You know I would never do anything to place my students in danger."

"Yes," agreed Commander Sisko. "I know how devoted you are to them. And despite their occasional problems, I think they're almost as devoted to you." He chuckled. "And after they hear about this trip, probably *more* devoted."

Jake could hardly wait until his teacher left. Then he immediately called Nog and told his Ferengi friend the great news. He was bubbling over with excitement at the

thought of finally getting to make a trip through the Wormhole and to a whole alien world in the Gamma Quadrant.

"Neat," agreed Nog. "That means we get out of a week of lessons. I like that." Trust Nog to think like that! He wasn't fond of school but went to be with his friends.

Jake called Ashley afterward to tell her. She was a lot

more positive, whooping and cheering. She signed off so that she could call T'Ara and give her the news. It was going to be a terrific trip, that was absolutely certain.

The following morning, however, things didn't seem to be quite as bright. When Jake met Nog on his way to class, the Ferengi boy had a deep scowl on his face. "What's wrong?" Jake asked.

"My uncle won't let me go on the trip," Nog complained. "He says it's a waste of time."

That was awful! Much as he wanted to go on the field trip, Jake knew it wouldn't be half as much fun if Nog couldn't come along, too. "Maybe he'll change his mind," he suggested hopefully.

"Uncle Quark?" Nog scoffed. "The only thing he ever changes are banknotes for coins." He gave a loud sigh. "I'm just gonna have to stay behind while you all have fun. And we'll probably get stuck with a substitute teacher like"—he shuddered at the thought—"Darl Tavros."

Jake shook his head desperately. "You've got to come along, Nog! It won't be the same if you don't! There's got to be a way to change your uncle's mind on this." Then he had an idea as he thought about what Nog had said. "I know how! What does your uncle love more than anything?"

"That's easy," said Nog. "Money. He's a good Ferengi." He sounded proud of his uncle.

"Then that's the way to go," Jake said, convinced he'd hit on the right strategy. "Come on." He led his skeptical friend back to his uncle's game rooms. Quark was there, overseeing getting the place in order for the day's business. Nog's father, Rom, was scuttling about working. Jake knew that it wouldn't make any difference appealing to Rom—he would never dare to disagree with any decisions that Quark made. As in all Ferengi families, the older brother made the rules for everyone.

Quark glanced up as Jake approached. "The answer's no, whatever the question is," he snapped. He was in his usual grouchy mood.

"But you haven't heard me!" protested Jake.

"I don't need to hear you," Quark replied. "There's nothing you could say that's of any interest to me." He turned his back on the two friends and concentrated on the PADD in his hand.

"Too bad," said Jake. "Sorry, Nog, I guess I'll have to make all the profit on my own on this one." He started to turn away.

As he'd expected, he didn't get far. Quark's hand shot out and grabbed his arm. "Profit?" he repeated. He gave his nephew a scowl. "You didn't mention anything about profit. I thought this was just some silly trip for that school of yours."

Jake shrugged. "I guess that's all it is, then," he said innocently.

"You can't fool me," Quark snapped. "Isn't this just some silly human thing—taking a holiday, going on vacation, that kind of thing? And to a world with nothing on it but plants? Not even any nice, profitable ruins filled with antiques."

"That's right," agreed Jake. "Nothing there but plants. Nothing for you to bother about."

Quark glared at him suspiciously. "So why are you so keen on going there?" he asked. "You're up to something, aren't you. I can smell it. So tell me!"

Jake gave an elaborate shrug. "I guess I'd better own up," he said. "Medicines."

"Medicines?" asked Quark. "What are you talking about? Are you sick?"

"No," Jake told him. "But you will be if you don't get in on this. What are most medicines developed from? Plants, right? And this is a whole world filled with plants that have never been tested for their medical value. I'll bet there are hundreds of plants on Cetus Beta that might have lifesaving drugs in them."

"Thousands," added Nog, catching on to the greedy look in his uncle's eye. "And nobody has a deal as yet for any of them."

Quark tried to cover up the greed in his voice. "As I was saying, Nog," he purred, "I think a little trip like this will do you a world of good. *Us* a world of good. Just be sure you bring back plenty of plant samples, won't you? I'm sure my place could do with some flowers to brighten it up."

Nog chuckled. "And what's my cut?" he asked.

"Our cut," corrected Jake. "It was *my* idea."

Quark considered. "Five percent," he finally said.

"Forget it," said Jake immediately. Ferengi never gave a good offer on the first try.

14

Quark sighed theatrically and squirmed. "Each," he added.

"Done," said Nog quickly. Grabbing Jake's arm, he led his friend away, grinning. "Not bad for a human. You got him to agree to me going *and* you may even make us some money off the trip."

"I could have gotten ten percent each if you hadn't rushed us out," complained Jake.

"From Uncle Quark?" scoffed Nog. "No way! You're not *that* good!"

CHAPTER 3

Ashley and even T'Ara seemed to be just as excited about the field trip as Jake and Nog. The four of them were thrilled to be getting out for a week on an alien world, and to actually go through the Wormhole. The only problem was that the next few days seemed to take forever to pass. Jake found it difficult to concentrate on his lessons with the thought of the trip always present in his mind.

Six of the Bajoran students were going with them. Marn Laren was their unofficial leader, since she was both two years older than the others and also by nature somewhat bossy. Jake and the others got along well enough with her, but they weren't part of that circle. The other five Bajorans were Taran Bakis, Bren Senor, Chel Boras (all boys), Rakt Loran, and Pahat Kalen, two more girls. Jake knew them all from school, but they were all under ten and too young to include in his normal activities. Ms. O'Brien had arranged for a substitute teacher to take on the four other students that weren't going along on the field trip. Two of them were too young, and the last two were going to be leaving the station in the next few days when their parents moved on.

On the last day before the trip Ms. O'Brien gave those four the afternoon off. For the remaining students, she had small tricorders that she handed out. "These will be very useful to you on the trip," she explained. "They've been programmed with all the information that you might need to know about Cetus Beta. I thought we should have a short talk before we leave about what you can expect." Tapping in commands on her computer desk, she called up a projection of a planet. It spun slowly about four feet from the ground and was the size of a large beachball. It was mostly blue, with a lot of green splotches across it.

"The planet is mostly water," their teacher explained. "There are thousands of islands all over the planet, most in long strings or chains. We'll be going to the largest one of these." It lit up a brighter shade of green for them. "There are no animals at all on the planet, but there are many, many forms of strange plant life, some of which look a bit like animals at first sight."

"Are any of them dangerous?" asked Ashley.

"Only to each other," Ms. O'Brien replied. "Some of them are like plant versions of lions and tigers, but they only eat other plants, of course. Since there has never been animal life on the planet, they tend to ignore visitors. Some of them can even move about pretty quickly, which could take some getting used to. I'm more accustomed to plants that stay in one spot!"

"So there's nothing harmful to worry about?" asked Jake. He wondered if that meant the planet might get a bit dull.

"I didn't say that," their teacher answered. "And I don't want you to think it for a moment. Just because nothing will *deliberately* try to harm you doesn't mean that everything is perfectly safe. For one thing, do *not* eat any of the plants unless you check with your tricorder first that it isn't poisonous. While nothing on the planet will kill you if you eat it, I can promise you that there are lots of plants that will make you so sick you'll wish you were dying. And then there are some of the very weird plants that you'd better just avoid." She tapped the computer again, and now a new projection appeared next to the spinning planet. It looked like a ball made of grass or rope.

"This was named a Tingle Tangler," she explained. Beside it, a tall, drooping plant appeared. At the end of each frond was a small Tingle Tangler. "It's one of the attack plants I mentioned earlier. When another plant gets close . . ." She tapped a command on her pad, and one of the small balls fell from the plant. As it did so, it seemed to explode. The larger model Tingle Tangler exploded, too, shooting out ropes like a net. "It wraps up its victim and then gives it a powerful electrical shock. This stuns the plant long enough for the Tingle Tangler to eat it."

"Would we get hurt by one of them?" asked T'Ara, clearly fascinated.

"Yes. It wouldn't kill you, but it would be very painful. And, as I say, the plant couldn't eat you. But you would be best to avoid going anywhere too close to one of these bushes. So you all must be careful on Cetus Beta."

"Yeah," grunted Taran Bakis. "I sure wouldn't want to have a plant try to eat me, then vomit me out." He shivered.

Marn Laren grinned. Bakis was a bit of a wimp. "Sounds like fun to me."

Ms. O'Brien nodded. "As long as everyone acts sensibly, it should be a lot of fun for us all."

Jake was getting really psyched up for the trip now. It did sound interesting, and it would be the first really alien planet he'd ever been on. Even though he'd been down to Bajor a few times and on other planets before he arrived on Deep Space Nine, they had all seemed very similar. They were all worlds where humans and other intelligent beings lived, with cities and most of the wilder spots pretty much tamed. This planet, on the other hand, sounded as if it was really a wild place. Plants that attacked each other and even ran around. This was going to be one neat trip!

Back in his room that evening Jake started packing stuff he'd need for the week. Clothing, of course, and a disk reader with a couple of book cubes. The tricorder he'd just been given. But what else? As he was wondering what he should add to the small pile, his father knocked softly on the door and entered.

"How's it going, Jake?" he asked. There was a smile tugging at his lips. "Getting excited about the trip?"

"You bet," agreed Jake happily. "This is going to be just terrific. A whole week on an alien planet! Uh . . . not that I won't miss you, Dad, but . . ."

His father laughed. "I know! I remember the first time I got to camp out on an alien world, too. It's a very special experience, and I know you and your friends are really going to enjoy it. Anyway, since it's your birthday in a few weeks, I thought I'd give you one of your presents early so you could take it along with you on this trip."

"Really?" asked Jake. This was getting better and better all the time. "Thanks, Dad!"

Commander Sisko chuckled and handed over a small silver vid-game projector. It was small enough to fit in Jake's lap, with two sets of hand controls and a computer pad set into the side. "I had it specially sent in for you," he explained. "It's a baseball program, with over ten thousand different plays in its memory."

"Hot stuff!" exclaimed Jake with real enthusiasm. Though baseball as a sport had died out a few hundred years earlier, he and his father shared a love of the game. Often they'd go to the holodeck to relive some really special games. Now, thanks to his father, he had a hologame of his own to play with!

"In case you get bored in the evenings," his father said. "Now you'll have something to keep you occu-

pied." He showed Jake how to start it up, and a six-inch-high batter appeared, followed by a catcher, a pitcher, and an umpire. "Key in the play you want, and you can take any position you like and then try the play. The second set of controls is if you want to take on another player. I'm sure you'll get the hang of it pretty fast." He then shut it off. "But no playing with it until you're all packed for the trip!"

"Okay," agreed Jake happily. He gave his father a hug. "Thanks, Dad. It's the coolest gift." He couldn't help grinning. "Boy, is this going to be the best trip ever!"

The following morning Jake met up with Nog outside Quark's Place. Nog had a backpack slung over his shoulder and a gleam in his eye. Despite his uncle's opinion that vacations were a human invention for wasting time and money, and not the kind of thing Ferengi enjoyed, Nog was obviously looking forward to the trip as much as Jake.

"I've got a dozen expandable sample containers," Nog told Jake. "Uncle Quark gave them to me as a gift and told me to bring back as many samples of the plants as I can." He rubbed his hands together. "I can almost smell the money we're going to make already! Boy, how much more fun could we have? A trip, time off from school, and a chance to make money. This is living!"

They hurried along together to the runabout pad. On the way, Ashley and T'Ara caught up with them. Both girls wore single-piece coveralls and had their long hair pulled back in braids. Jake supposed it was their idea of how explorers were supposed to dress. Ashley was flushed with excitement. T'Ara was trying her best to look composed and unemotional about the trip, but there was a gleam in her eye and she seemed to be almost ready to jump up and down from happiness. The four of them compared notes on what they'd packed as they made their way to the pad.

There the ship was waiting for them. Its name—the *Orinoco*—was painted on the prow, and several engineers were performing last minute checks on it. Ms. O'Brien was there already, checking on supplies that were being stowed aboard. Her young daughter, Molly, was with her, watching everything with her intense stare. As the four students approached the ship, the teacher looked around.

"You can go aboard now," she told them. "Take your pick of the seats and stow your bags. As soon as I finish up here, we'll be ready to go, okay?"

"Sure enough," agreed Jake. He led the others into the runabout through the open door in the side, and then looked around.

To the left was the prow and the special module insert with the flight seats. There were twenty of these, arranged in pairs on either side of an aisle. To the right was the storage room where the supplies were being loaded. Beyond that must be the engines.

"Front seats!" said Ashley with excitement. She hurried down the aisle and laid claim to one of the seats on the left at the front of the passenger cabin. T'Ara grabbed the one beside her. Jake and Nog took the two seats across the aisle. There were small lockers under the seats for their bags, which they immediately stowed away.

There was a row of windows down the side of the craft, through which they could see the activity in the launch bay. The flight deck was directly in front of them, with three seats set in front of the flight computers. Only one of these was occupied; obviously this was the person who was to be their pilot, and the only other adult along on the trip. Hearing the sounds of movement behind him, the man twisted in his seat to look back. He was a tall man, wearing the pips on his collar to show he was a Starfleet lieutenant. He had a mess of straw-colored hair and a thin, somewhat nervous face.

"Keep it down back there, okay?" he called. "I'd appreciate it."

Jake shrugged. "Okay," he agreed. Not that they had been noisy anyway, but it was better not to argue.

"Fine." The lieutenant turned back to his checks, but Jake distinctly heard him mutter: "Children should be seen and not heard." Ashley had obviously heard it, too, because she stuck out her tongue at the man's back.

"Children," she said softly. She made it sound as if she were cursing. "I don't think we're gonna get along too well with this guy."

Jake tried to pretend he wasn't bothered, but he didn't like being called a child, either. Still, this trip was too important to start it by arguing with their pilot. Instead,

Jake peered through the small window beside his seat. "Here come the others," he said.

Marn Laren led her little group of Bajorans into the craft. She looked a little annoyed that the four friends had already claimed the front seats. However, she was too excited by the thought of the trip to kick up a fuss, and she soon had the six of them installed in the next two rows. The other Bajorans looked eager, except for Taran Bakis. Nervous as ever, he was almost shaking.

"I don't want to go," he muttered.

"Show some spirit," Laren told him, annoyed. "We're Bajorans. Nothing scares us."

"I gotta go to the bathroom," Bakis answered and rushed to the back of the craft. Laren sighed.

Their pilot glanced back as the Bajorans were stowing their packs and chattering happily. "Keep it down," he called. "I'm trying to work up here. Okay?"

Laren scowled back at him. "We're doing our best," she snapped. "Give us a break, will you?"

Before the pilot could reply, Ms. O'Brien entered the shuttle carrying Molly. Both of them were grinning. "Everybody happy?" she asked.

"Not everybody," T'Ara said with blunt honesty. She glanced at the pilot.

Ms. O'Brien placed Molly in one of the seats that was still empty and then looked at the pilot. "Is something wrong, Lieutenant Danvers?" she asked mildly.

The pilot thought for a moment, and then shook his head. "Just kids," he said. "They're kind of noisy for my liking."

"Well," Mrs. O'Brien replied, "I'm afraid you'll have to get used to slightly increased noise levels for the next week. Believe me, it is possible to adjust. I had to."

"If you say so," Lieutenant Danvers said politely. He gestured to his panel. "Well, ma'am, we appear to be about ready. Everything looks good from here, and the stores are all stowed."

"Marvelous," the teacher answered. She took one of the two free seats beside the pilot as Bakis returned to his seat. "Shall we get under way?"

"Okay," he agreed. He tapped in several quick commands. Jake heard the outer door hiss closed and the seals snap on. The interior lighting of the shuttle brightened slightly. The pilot said: "Life support, all green. Internal gravity normal. Power levels full." He tapped his communicator badge. *"Orinoco* to Ops; awaiting clearance."

"Ops to runabout *Orinoco,"* came Commander Sisko's voice from the air. "You're cleared to leave." There was the slightest pause and then: "Have a great time. That's an order. Sisko out."

Jake leaned forward in his seat, staring through the transparent window at the front of the craft. There was a soft whine, conducted through the floor, and he could see that the ship was rising. The gravity inside the ship was kept constant, so there was no sensation of movement at all, but Jake knew that the airlock overhead must have slid open and the ram below the runabout was pushing the craft upward.

Then the stars appeared as they cleared the upper deck

of the station. The younger Bajorans all gasped and laughed at the sight of the millions of stars burning brightly in the sky. The bulk of the station was below them, and one of the pylons ahead and to the right. A light blinked on and off atop it.

"Here we go," said Lieutenant Danvers. At his gentle touch the runabout's engines whined slightly more loudly, and the ship rose from the docking ram and into free space.

Their field trip had begun!

CHAPTER 4

Jake pressed his face against the window beside him, determined not to miss anything that happened. He did steal one quick glance about the cabin, though, to make sure he wasn't the only one acting so excitedly. To his relief, everyone else was staring avidly out the windows closest to them. Even Nog was crowding him a bit in order to get the best view.

So far they had seen nothing that couldn't be witnessed every day from the station itself. However, Jake knew that in a few moments that would all change. They were approaching the Wormhole.

Normally the Wormhole was invisible. This was how it had remained undiscovered for so long, until Jake's father had made the first trip into it over two years earlier. Now that its position was known precisely, the runabout could take the same approach path that would trigger the visual outpouring of the Wormhole.

"Here we go," called Ms. O'Brien from her seat. She

sounded almost as excited as Jake felt. He glanced across the cabin and saw the stars through the large front window suddenly—

Explode in a barrage of light!

The Wormhole was like a huge whirlpool of all imaginable colors, swirling and glowing in space right in front of the runabout. Several of the students gave gasps of delight, and Molly cried: "Pretty!" Jake couldn't blame her: It *was* the most beautiful sight imaginable.

And then the small craft flew into the mouth of the Wormhole, and the stars vanished completely. All about the ship was a solid mass of colors—reds, blues, greens, yellows, purples—in all shades and combinations. It was as if someone had taken millions of shades of all the colors of the spectrum and then whipped them all together and threw the resulting mess onto the wall of a giant spinning tunnel. Lights within the wall glowed and skipped, highlighting portions of the swirling complex of colors. It was an unimaginable result, and Jake stared at it in awe. He knew that the colors were a product of the warped space on the particles of light that traveled through the Wormhole, but that was just the facts. The brilliant, almost hypnotic, whirlpool of colors was simply beautiful.

He also knew that this Wormhole was artificial. It had been created by a race of alien beings that lived outside of time itself. They allowed other races to use it, but they very rarely contacted anyone who traveled this path.

The runabout plowed onward. It looked as if Lieutenant Danvers was threading them down a long and

winding pathway that ran through the tunnel of color, but Jake knew that they were actually being pulled along by the Wormhole itself, which was tugging them through to its far end. The trip seemed to take forever, but actually lasted only about five minutes. But what five minutes! It was just incredible, staring out at the tunnel.

Then they were through it, and the stars suddenly reappeared about them. Molly said: "Awww!" and the other students all sighed. Jake was a little disappointed, but also a little relieved. Staring so long at the swirling colors had started his head spinning, too. He caught one last glimpse of the whirlpool of light, and the Wormhole closed behind them, and they were in the Gamma Quadrant at last.

"Oh, wow," he breathed, settling back into his seat. "That was some trip!"

Nog sat down properly and wrinkled his nose. "It was okay, I guess," he said, obviously trying not to sound too impressed.

"Okay?" asked Ashley. "It was *awesome!* Right, T'Ara?"

The young Vulcan girl nodded solemnly. "Most . . . enlightening." Jake wondered if that was her idea of a pun, but knew that even if it was, she'd never admit to having a sense of humor.

"I feel sick," said Bakis from behind them.

"Oh, grow up!" snapped Laren.

Ms. O'Brien came back to join them. "The rest of the journey is going to take us about three hours at warp speed," she said. "So don't get too impatient." She glanced back over her shoulder in the direction of the pilot. "Or too noisy, okay? Maybe you should all take the chance to go over the notes in your tricorders about Cetus Beta so you'll know some more about it by the time we arrive."

Jake wished he could play with his vid-game instead, but he knew a gentle order when he heard one. They might be off school for the next week, but that didn't mean that they weren't going to have to do some studying, obviously!

"There we are," announced Lieutenant Danvers finally. He gestured ahead of the small craft at the planet hanging in the blackness of space. It looked to Jake almost identical to the hologram that he'd seen in class—a globe slowly moving, mostly blue, with blotches of green that were islands. The only difference was that this real world had trails of clouds across it. "Okay, kids, get back in your seats," the lieutenant added. "This should be a real smooth landing, but let's not chance any broken bones, okay?"

Jake felt the slight tug of the forcefield that held him in his seat. He knew that the internal gravity field of the runabout should make it simple to land, but their pilot was probably right to take no chances. If they ran into a storm, things could get bumpy.

"Isn't this great?" he asked Nog excitedly.

The Ferengi shrugged, again pretending he wasn't impressed. "I guess so."

"I think it's really neat," Ashley commented. "This is going to be the first alien world I've ever been on, except for Bajor! I can hardly wait to go exploring."

"Yeah," agreed Bren Senor, who was sitting behind her. "And Bajor isn't alien; it's home."

"Maybe for you," Ashley said with a laugh.

The globe ahead of them had grown in size as they approached it, and now overflowed the windows. Lieutenant Danvers was bringing the runabout easily down toward the world. Through the large window, Jake could see nothing now but ocean and the scattered strings of islands. One of them was their target, and they'd be down in a few minutes.

"That's odd," muttered the pilot suddenly. He glanced at Ms. O'Brien. "I'm getting a lot of static on the sensors."

"Trouble?" she asked, worried.

"I don't think so," he replied. "It won't affect our landing, but these readings are very odd. It's like there's—" He broke off. "There's another ship, coming up from the planet!"

"There isn't supposed to be anybody else here," the teacher replied. "I checked. So what are they doing?" She leaned over the sensor computer and started to scan the readings. "Do we have an identification yet?"

"No, the interference is making it— It's a Cardassian raider!"

Jake and the rest couldn't help hearing all of this conversation. He suddenly felt sick. While the Cardassians were supposed to be at peace with the

Federation, they could get nasty at times. They were a very aggressive race, and the military ruled their worlds. These soldiers didn't care much for the uneasy peace with the Federation and often strained it to almost the breaking point. If the Cardassians were here on Cetus Beta for some unexplained reason, then they wouldn't be likely to want any members of the Federation around.

"Oh, great," he muttered. "Maybe they've decided to claim this planet and want us to go home. That could ruin the trip."

"And our hopes of making money," agreed Nog with a groan.

In the cabin Ms. O'Brien glanced quickly back at her students. "Maybe we should call for help?" she suggested softly.

"Can't at the moment," Lieutenant Danvers replied. "The static's too strong. Still, I don't think that even the Cardassians would try and cause trouble. Would they?"

"I'll try hailing them and see what they want," Ms. O'Brien said. "It's probably nothing serious." She reached toward the communicator panel, but she didn't get a chance even to try.

There was a bright flash directly in front of the craft, and the runabout gave a series of shudders. Several of the younger Bajorans screamed, and Jake was blinded for a second.

"They're firing on us!" the pilot cried, astounded. "The dirty little . . ." His fingers flew over the controls as he tried to regain level heading once more.

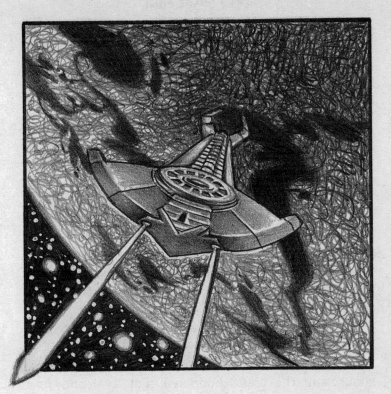

The seat's forcefield held Jake firmly in place; otherwise he'd have been thrown across the cabin. A couple of
tricorders and several smaller items were slamming back
and forth. Bakis was screaming, and Molly had begun to
howl in response. There was nothing he could do to help
them, since he could barely shift in his seat.

A second soundless blast shook the runabout, and this

time there was a smell of burning from the rear of the cabin. Jake managed to look over his shoulder and saw sparks flying out of the supply area.

"We've been hit!" Lieutenant Danvers yelled.

"How badly?" asked Ms. O'Brien, her face pale.

"Hard to say," the pilot answered tightly. He was struggling with the controls as the runabout shook from side to side. "I'm gonna try for a landing. We're still on course for that large island, at least."

Jake wished there was something he could do. Even if the forcefield wasn't holding him in place, though, he knew that he'd only get in the way. On the other hand, he might be able to comfort some of the younger kids. Bakis was still screaming in fear, and now Chel Boras and Pahat Kalen had joined in. Molly was crying and shaking. Jake reached back and held her hand.

"I'm gonna die," muttered Nog. "Worse—I'm gonna die *poor!*"

There was a screaming noise from outside the runabout, and the craft shuddered. For a second Jake thought they'd been hit again, but then he realized it was because the ship had entered the planet's atmosphere and there was air outside to conduct sound—and create turbulence.

"Hang on!" yelled Lieutenant Danvers. "This is gonna be a real bumpy landing, I'm afraid."

Jake could see the planet below filling the forward window now. They seemed to be heading down toward it awfully fast. From the side window he could see a trail of smoke. Something had to be burning or venting outside the craft. He could only hope it was nothing essential, like the braking thrusters. . . . His heart was racing, and in the back of his mind was the knowledge that they might not survive the landing attempt.

Then the island filled the forward view. It was huge and absolutely covered with plants, trees, and other greenery. Cliffs loomed ahead of them, but somehow the pilot brought the nose of the runabout up, and they avoided smashing into the cliff face. Huge towers of rocks whipped past the small ship, and below them was a tangle of jungle.

Lieutenant Danvers was hitting the control panels to try and get responses. Several of them had small fires that Ms. O'Brien was trying to put out with a foam extinguisher. Then, finally, the braking jets kicked in. If it hadn't been for the gravity field holding up, Jake and the others would have been slammed into their seats with enough force to break their spines. As it was, he was still shaken by the sudden loss of forward motion.

There was the unmistakable sound of another explosion outside the ship. A huge chunk of the exterior peeled away from the craft, scratched along the window beside Jake, and then plunged to the ground below. A fireball belched out from the side of the ship.

"Losing power!" the pilot called. "We're goin' in!"

The runabout lurched again, and the nose dropped. Jake almost lost his breakfast. The craft plunged down toward the tangled greenery below. Nog was shaking in

fear, his face buried in his arms, but Jake couldn't look away. The trees were suddenly right in front of the ship.

Metal screamed and tore; branches were ripped free and pulped. The runabout shook like one of the millions of leaves that were flying from the impact. One window toward the back of the craft shattered, showering transparent aluminum into the runabout.

There were further explosions from the back of the ship, and then the artificial gravity field died. Jake's stomach wrenched as the planet's gravity took over. The craft slammed hard against a huge tree that had to be almost fifty feet across its trunk. The collision shattered the front window and ripped a huge tear in the trunk. Jake was hammered in his seat by the force of the impact, and he almost blacked out. He heard Lieutenant Danvers give a scream of pain, and then the runabout fell heavily the final few feet to the ground.

CHAPTER 5

For a few seconds there was silence. It was broken almost at the same time by the sound of another small explosion from the rear of the runabout and by the sound of Molly bawling at the top of her voice.

Jake shook himself, knowing he had bruises all over from the battering he'd taken as the runabout had come to rest. He glanced at Nog, who still had his head buried in his arms. "Hey, you're alive," he told his friend.

Nog glanced up. "Yeah," he agreed. "But I'm still poor." Jake realized it was a weak attempt at humor to ward off panic.

Looking around, Jake saw that the small craft was in bad shape. The ceiling at the back had caved in, and there was a branch sticking through the hole, dripping thick, yellow sap into a growing pool. There was a small fire crackling away back there. At a quick count it looked as if Bakis, Kalen, and Boras were all unconscious—knocked out or fainted. Ashley and T'Ara were shaken, and T'Ara had a cut down her cheek that was slowly leaking her greenish blood. The front of the craft—

It was a mess. It had borne the brunt of the impact. The window was gone, except for the mess on the floor. Luckily it was designed to shatter harmlessly if breached rather than into shards that could hurt or kill. Ms. O'Brien was okay, it seemed. She was moving, and pushing her dark hair back from her face. Lieutenant Danvers, though, was in real bad shape. He'd slammed into the control panel when the crash had happened, and the panel had shattered. There was blood on his face and his left arm. And there was a long gash down his left leg that was dripping dark blood to the floor.

Luckily, Jake had taken a course in emergency first aid back on DS9. Dr. Bashir had insisted on it for one of their classes. Jake knew that the most urgent thing was to stop that bleeding before the pilot died. The forcefields holding the passengers in their seats had cut off immediately after the crash. Jake staggered to his feet. His head spun for a moment, but then he forced himself to move. He stumbled toward the nose of the ship.

Ms. O'Brien beat him to the wounded pilot. She'd ripped the sleeve off her tunic and was using it as a tourniquet on Lieutenant Danvers's leg to stop the flow of blood. Then she glanced up and saw Jake. "We've got to get everyone off the ship," she said. Her voice was shaking a little, but she sounded firm. "There's no telling if it's going to explode."

Jake nodded. He turned to find Ashley, T'Ara, and Nog staggering toward them. "We've got to get out," he told them, leaving his teacher to look after the pilot. "Ashley, you want to try opening the door with me?"

"I will check the others," T'Ara said. "Come on, Nog."

Leading the way over the wreckage in the aisle, Jake made it to the exit door. It had buckled under the impact, and he wondered if it was too twisted to open properly. He slapped the panel, but nothing happened.

"The power lines have been severed," Ashley told him. "I don't think any of the ship's systems will work."

"Great." Jake sighed. He opened the small panel for the manual control. There didn't seem to be any damage inside it, and he grabbed the small handle in the recess. With a tug he activated the system and then waited.

There was a loud groaning sound, and the door cracked open. It shivered and shook but couldn't manage to open all the way. When it stopped, there was a gap large enough for them to clamber through at least. "We'd better start getting everyone out," he told Ashley. "I'll go first and check. You get the others moving." Ashley nodded.

Jake slid through the small opening and onto the ground. He'd been really excited before about stepping onto an alien planet, but right now he was more worried than anything else. Could they get everyone away from the shuttle in case it blew up? How far would they have to go to be safe? What could they take with them? Was there any shelter?

He looked around. There were trees, bushes, plants, flowers, mosses—all around there was a curtain and carpet of greenery, except for the huge gash where the runabout had skidded when it had crashed. There the soil was torn, and the trees felled. It was almost impossible to see more than about ten or twenty meters in any direction because the plants were so thick and tall. There was simply no telling what lay in any direction.

"Is it okay?" called Ashley from inside the ship.

"I guess," he replied. "It's got to be safer out here than in there. But we'll need tricorders to get any idea which way to go."

"Right." Ashley disappeared from view, and her place was taken by Nog.

"Ready?" he asked but didn't wait for a reply. Instead he almost pushed Kalen out of the gap. "Come on, move it," he snapped. "I don't want to stay here, you know."

Jake helped the young girl out, and Senor took her place. One by one the Bajoran children came out. The three who'd been unconscious were still looking pretty shaken, but they were able to function at least. Then came Molly, who was now quiet, thankfully. Tears weren't far away, though, so she seemed to be taking just a short rest. The last of the Bajorans out was Marn Laren. She was pale and had a nasty-looking gash down the side of her forehead.

"How do you feel?" Jake asked her as she stumbled to the ground beside him.

"I'll live," she snapped, with some of her normal ferocity. "Provided we get away from this ship. Bajorans are tough, you know."

T'Ara jumped lightly to the ground. She was holding

two tricorders and handed one to Jake. The other she opened immediately and began scanning their surroundings. Nog followed her out of the craft, his backpack slung over one shoulder and Jake's slung over the other.

"Why are we hanging about?" he growled. "Let's get away from this thing, fast!"

"When we know where to go," Jake said. He looked to T'Ara for an answer.

The Vulcan girl pointed. "There is a small range of mountains in that direction," she announced. "I can detect some signs of caves, which would provide shelter. They are at most a kilometer away."

"Great," Jake replied. "You and Nog—and Laren!" he added quickly, lest the Bajoran girl get annoyed. "Take the younger ones up there. I'll see what's keeping Ashley and the others."

"Affirmative," T'Ara agreed.

For a moment it looked as if Laren would complain about him giving orders, but she shrugged and followed the Vulcan. "Makes sense," she agreed. "Come on, guys."

"I'm scared," complained Bakis, sniffling.

"Be scared, then," Laren told him. "Just don't show it. We're Bajorans, remember. Preserve your dignity."

Nog hefted the two packs. "Better not hang about too long," he said to Jake. "Uh—if you're killed in there, I'll look after your stuff."

Sell it for a profit, thought Jake. But there was no point in getting annoyed with the way Nog was; he couldn't help his Ferengi nature. Jake nodded and then clambered back inside the damaged ship.

The emergency lighting was flickering, obviously about to fail, but there was enough light from outside to show Jake that the craft was in bad shape indeed. Ms. O'Brien and Ashley were half carrying and half dragging Lieutenant Danvers toward the door. Jake hurried to help them. The pilot was unconscious and breathing heavily. His leg was patched with cloth torn from an emergency blanket.

"The others have gone on ahead," he reported to his teacher. "Do we have time to try and get some supplies?"

Ms. O'Brien shook her head. "I'd rather not risk it," she said. "The supplies are too close to the reactor, and it may explode. Let's just get away from here for now."

Together, the three of them managed to get the unconscious pilot through the doorway. Once outside, Jake and Ms. O'Brien took an arm each over their shoulders. Using her tricorder, Ashley quickly discovered the way that the other students had gone. Jake was just glad to be heading away from the damaged shuttle. He had to resist the urge to keep looking back over his shoulder, and to fight the fear that it might blow up any second and kill them.

It was tough going through the jungle. There was a path of sorts, but not a good one. There weren't any animals here to make real trails, Jake realized, and so this one must have been caused some other way. Maybe some of those mobile plants that lived here? Everywhere they traveled, green things surrounded them. Trees towered eighty feet or higher, trailing leaves and creepers. Bushes and shrubs were all around those, and then lower down what looked like ferns. There was no grass or anything like that, but there was a layer of what seemed to be some sort of moss over the ground.

Amid all of that, there were flowers and fruits of all sizes, shapes, and colors. It was incredible walking through all the lush life. There were hundreds of different scents in the air, but no real perfumes from the flowers. Perfume was, after all, just a trick by flowers to get insects to pollinate them, and there were no insects on this world. He wondered why there were so many colors, in that case, with no insects to attract. Maybe just random? Or did some of the plants have eyes of some kind that could see colors?

Finally the ground seemed to rise a bit under their feet, and Jake could see flashes of gray and brown rocks through gaps in the trees. They were nearly at the foot of the mountains—which were still almost invisible because of all the plant life!

There was a welcoming cry from ahead of them, and then Ashley waved. "T'Ara's up there," she reported. This gave Jake a little extra strength, and a few moments later they broke through a gap in the vegetation. There was a small clearing ahead of them, moss-covered but free of other plants. Beyond this was the mouth of a sizable cave. T'Ara was in the entrance, waving. As they drew closer, Jake saw that the other students were inside, most of them sitting down or lying on the ground. He didn't blame them; most must be still shaken after the crash, and even though it hadn't been a really long walk here, they were quite young.

Ms. O'Brien gently lowered Lieutenant Danvers to the ground once they were inside the cave. She had a backpack slung across her own shoulders, Jake suddenly noticed. From it she pulled an emergency blanket. It was very thin, but he knew it would be warm and comfortable. Ashley helped them, and they managed to get the injured pilot wrapped up inside the blanket.

"Is he gonna be okay?" Ashley asked the teacher.

Ms. O'Brien sighed. "I wish I knew. He's lost a lot of blood and banged his head. He might have a concussion." She pulled a medical kit from her bag. "I did have time to get this, but I'm not sure I know how to use it properly." She pulled out a medical tricorder and scanned the pilot. She didn't say what it showed her, but Jake saw her frown. Then she looked up. "How are the others?"

"Mostly okay, I guess," Laren told her. "Bruises and cuts, that's all."

Ms. O'Brien nodded. "I'd better check everyone, just the same." She scooped up Molly into her arms. "How's my sweetheart?" she asked her daughter. Molly didn't answer but clung to her mother. Jake saw Ms. O'Brien use the tricorder on her, then give a smile. She moved off, still with Molly clutching tightly to her, to check out the others.

Jake stared back down the hill toward the spot where

their ship had crashed. There was nothing but trees and plants to be seen, of course. Something large and green skittered across the small clearing and vanished. He shook his head; this place was *strange*. Still, he'd not heard an explosion, and there was no sign of smoke or fire. Maybe the shuttle was going to be okay.

Ashley, T'Ara, and Nog joined him in the cave entrance. The Vulcan girl was still scanning about with her tricorder. "It is most odd," she announced.

"What is?" asked Jake.

"The Cardassians."

Nog snorted. "You can't trust them," he growled. "What's odd about them attacking us?"

"Everything," Jake said. "They aren't usually *that* nasty. And they must have known we didn't power up any weapons systems. We didn't even have time to raise shields before they attacked. Cardassians don't usually try and blow up bystanders."

"That is part of it," agreed T'Ara solemnly. "If they felt threatened by us for some reason, they might have tried to capture us, but not kill us. Still, what is most puzzling is that they did not kill us."

"Talk English," Ashley suggested.

"I mean," T'Ara explained, "that they had two or perhaps three passes in which to strike at our shuttle. Yet they missed hitting us on the first shot, and the second shot only damaged the ship. Surely the Cardassians are better shots than that? Why did they not blow us up?"

"Are you complaining?" argued Nog.

"No; merely—" She broke off as a loud scream suddenly came from the jungle ten feet away from them. It was a weird, echoing, terrifying sound that made Jake shudder.

CHAPTER 6

What is it?" Jake asked anxiously.

"*Who* is it?" corrected Ashley. She looked worried. "That's somebody screaming in agony!"

Nog grabbed Jake's arm. "Agony? That means pain! And I'm allergic to pain! It must be the Cardassians! They followed us!" he howled.

Prying lose his friend's fingers, Jake shook his head. "If it's them, then why would they scream and let us know they were coming?"

"To try and scare us!" Nog suggested.

"It worked," muttered Ashley, shivering. She glanced at T'Ara, who was studying the tricorder. "Haven't you got that figured out yet?"

T'Ara raised an eyebrow. "According to the readings," she said, "there *are* Cardassians out there, but a long way off. Almost a dozen kilometers, in fact. And apart from them, there's just those of us here in the cave."

The screaming was coming closer. Jake shook his

head. "Don't tell me that's just a figment of our imagina-
tions!"

"On the contrary," T'Ara replied. "It is definitely real.
But it is not a human being. Logically, it must be another
plant."

"A plant that *screams?*" Jake could hardly believe it.
This was one weird planet!

Even as he said it, something came hurtling out of the
bushes to the left of the clearing and rolled across the
mosses. It was ball-shaped, about a meter across, green,
leafy, and screaming at the top of its . . . well, *voice,* Jake
guessed. It looked like a gigantic cabbage and sounded
like a cat being murdered.

To his surprise, Nog suddenly darted after the rolling
ball. With a well-timed jump he landed atop the
cabbage-thing and scooped it up. The plant howled even
louder at this indignity as Nog marched back to the cave
with it in triumph. "My first specimen," he told Jake.
"Neat, eh?"

"Noisy," Ashley corrected, covering her ears. "If it
keeps that noise up, there's no way I'm gonna let you
keep it anywhere near me. It's giving *me* the screaming
mimis!"

"No problem." Nog whipped out a small, leathery
pouch from his backpack. He managed to push the
cabbage-thing into it, then tapped a small control pad on
the outside of the pouch. The leather instantly sealed
over, and the howling ceased. Nog flashed a wide grin at
his friends. "Stasis pouch," he explained. "That'll keep

the thing fresh—and quiet—till we get back home." He gave Ashley a smug smile. "I think I'll call this thing a Screaming Mimi. I like the sound of it." Then he added: "The name, not the plant!"

Jake turned back to T'Ara. "What about those readings for the Cardassians?" he asked her. "What do you think they're doing?"

The Vulcan girl studied the tricorder again. "There are six of them," she replied. "Two are inside some sort of craft on the ground; the other four are moving away from it."

"The ship that shot us down," Ashley guessed. "It must have landed, and now they're looking for us."

T'Ara raised an eyebrow. "It is not logical," she said. "If my tricorder can register them, then they should be able to locate us with their tricorders."

An idea occurred to Jake. "Maybe they don't *have* tricorders for some reason," he said slowly. "You said it was odd that they didn't manage to shoot us down when they attacked. Now they don't seem to be able to find us or the crashed runabout on the ground. It sounds like they're working under a handicap, doesn't it?"

"Agreed," T'Ara said. "It would explain also why they didn't attack us until we were quite close to the planet. But why would they not have even a simple sensor?"

"I don't know," admitted Jake. "This whole thing is pretty weird." As he said this, there was a wild thrashing sound from the jungle, followed by some very deep gurgling noises. He had no desire to find out what had caused the sounds. Jake headed back farther into the cave, where Ms. O'Brien was examining the wounded pilot again. Lieutenant Danvers was asleep, but his breathing sounded very rough and his skin was really pale. "How is he?" he asked the teacher.

Ms. O'Brien sighed. "Bad, I'm afraid. He really needs medical attention, not just my attempts at doctoring with this travel kit." She stood up slowly, hugging Molly to her chest. "The other students are okay, though, and Molly and I are fine." She glanced around the cave. "We should be okay in here," she said. "But we'll need some food for everyone."

Ashley and the others had followed. Now the blond girl smiled. "No problem," she said. "We've still got our tricorders, so we can gather safe fruits and stuff to eat."

"Good idea," agreed Laren, hefting her own tricorder. "We can help, too."

"We could go back to the runabout and get some supplies," Jake offered.

Ms. O'Brien shook her head. "I'd rather not risk that for the moment. The engines might still explode. Let's give it a couple of hours before anyone ventures back there." She gave them an encouraging smile. "We'll be okay, I'm sure."

T'Ara gave a slight frown. "The Cardassians have landed on this island, too," she said in a low voice so the younger children wouldn't hear her. "They appear to be searching for us. If they come in this direction, they may be here in the morning."

The teacher paled at this news. "Then we really have to get a message out for help somehow," she said. "But how?"

"I think I can do it."

Jake looked down at Lieutenant Danvers, who had opened his eyes. The pilot was grimacing in pain, but struggled to prop himself up on one elbow. "The subspace transmitter on the runabout wasn't badly damaged in the crash," he said, gasping a little as he spoke. "It can be detached from the ship and has its own power core. If you bring it here with my tool kit from the supply cabinet, I'm sure I can rig up a distress call."

"But that means going back to the runabout!" exclaimed Ms. O'Brien. "That's very dangerous, surely?"

"It may not be." The pilot tried to rise, but fell back with a ground. "I can't make it," he apologized. "But I can rig a tricorder so that it can scan for signs that the engines may explode. That way it'll be less risky."

"I'll go," said Ashley and Jake together.

"I can't let you," the teacher replied, but there was a note of uncertainty in her voice. "I'll do it."

"You'd never be able to unhook the transmitter," said Ashley. "I know how to do it, and I'm a terrific engineer."

"And if the four of us go together," added Jake, "we can work faster and also get some of the supplies from the ship to bring back."

"Four?" Nog echoed. "What's with the four? I'm not going!"

"Yes, you are," Jake told him. "Anything on the wrecked ship is now salvage." He could see in his friend's eyes the thought of making money waging war with his fear, but he knew which would win out. He handed his tricorder to Lieutenant Danvers. "Here. You can recallibrate my tricorder, and I'll use it to keep watch on the engines."

"I'll come along, too," said Ms. O'Brien.

"You are needed here," T'Ara said. "The children will need your attention—and Molly. Also, you are the only one who can doctor Lieutenant Danvers should he get worse. We will be very careful."

"I'll come along," Laren said.

Jake shook his head. "You'd be more use if you organized your friends to hunt for food here, just in case we can't rescue enough supplies."

Laren thought this over, and then nodded. "Okay, that makes sense," she agreed. She crossed to the other Bajorans. "Okay, shape up. Bakis, *please* stop that sniveling, or I'll give you something to really howl about."

Ms. O'Brien looked at Jake and his friends, clearly worried. Finally she nodded. "All right—be *really* careful. Any sign of trouble, and I want you to come straight back. Don't do anything foolish, okay?"

"Don't worry," Jake promised. "We'll watch it. We know it's dangerous." He was a little scared at the thought of going back to the crash site, because he knew there was a chance they could get killed. At the same time he knew that they had to risk it—and there was a tingle of excitement added because of the risk. Because no matter how dangerous it was, it was their only hope of rescue.

CHAPTER 7

The four of them set out for the shuttle. Jake led the way, his tricorder at the ready. It was showing the runabout ahead of them, with a steady light pulse registering the energy of the engines. If the color started to shift into red from the yellow it now registered, then they would have to run for their lives. At the moment, though, there was no sign of such a change.

The noises of the jungle echoed strangely about them as they traveled. There were plants everywhere. Not an inch of ground was left uncovered, and there were many plants growing on top of others, and even twisted about the branches of the trees. Once they heard another Screaming Mimi rushing through the bushes, howling away. Nog had brought along his sample bags and took the opportunity to store another two samples—one a very pretty orchidlike flower of delicate lilac and gold coloring; the other a tall plant with blue bell-like flowers.

They passed close to one of the Tingle Tanglers, but thanks to their teacher's earlier lesson they were able to avoid trouble. The dangling leathery balls swayed slowly in the breeze, ready to spring into action.

As they walked, T'Ara kept up her scanning for Cardassians. The four searchers were still a number of kilometers away, but getting slightly closer all the time. Jake guessed that they'd seen the rough direction that the runabout had come down in and were now trying to narrow it down. Obviously they didn't have any tricorders or sensor capabilities, because the energy readings he was detecting from the runabout should have shown up for the Cardassians, too. It was very odd that they should be without such basic pieces of equipment, but Jake didn't know what to make of it.

"It's kind of pretty here, isn't it?" Ashley commented. "If we weren't stranded and being hunted, it would be a nice place for a field trip."

"Yeah," Jake agreed. "But we *are* stranded, and we *are* being hunted. I can't wait to get out of here!" Then he frowned. "That's odd."

"What?" She peered over his shoulder at the tricorder screen he was studying.

The yellow indicator light on the panel was fading slowly to white. "That is," he told her. "It looks as if the power level is dying down."

"So what's odd about it?" asked Ashley. "It's probably just cooling down instead of blowing up. It means it'll be safer for us to go into the ship, that's all."

"Yeah," agreed Jake doubtfully. "But it just started to change, and it was steady before."

"Maybe one of the plants got into the ship," suggested Nog. "And drained the energy." Seeing Ashley's blank look, he added: "A *power* plant!" He chuckled at his own joke.

"It just seems odd," Jake muttered. Again, though, he didn't know what it meant. This planet was getting stranger by the minute, it seemed.

T'Ara gave him an encouraging smile, then remembered she was a Vulcan and not supposed to do that. "We shall be there in about ten minutes," she told him, her face impassive again. "Then we shall see."

They moved on, drawing closer to the ship. The warning light on his tricorder was pure white now. It meant either that the engines had shut off completely or the tricorder was broken. He ran a diagnostic test on it, but it showed the device in working order. So why had the engine just shut down?

There was a rustling in the bushes to the side of the trail. Probably just another of those restless plants moving about again, but Jake's eyes flashed over the foliage. Then he stopped dead in his tracks.

For just the most fleeting of instants, he saw *something* in the shrubbery, peering back at him. Then it was gone. He didn't get a good look at it, but it was short, hairy . . . and humanoid.

"There's somebody there!" he cried, pointing.

"What?" The other three spun to stare where he

gestured, but there was now no sign of anything, and the only sounds were the leaves rustling in the wind.

T'Ara whipped up her tricorder and scanned. "I do not register any life forms other than plants," she replied.

Nog grimaced. "You *know* there's nothing but plants here," he complained. "Except for us and Cardassians— and they're kilometers away."

"I saw something," Jake insisted.

Nog wrinkled his nose in disgust. "Maybe you hit your head when we crashed," he said. "There's nothing out there. There *can't* be."

"I don't care," Jake replied. "I *did* see something in those bushes." He moved off the trail to take a closer look. But there was nothing there now, and no marks on the moss-covered ground, either. Uncertainly, he looked back at his friends.

Nog rolled his eyes. "You gonna play games, or are we going to scavenge the ship?"

"Okay." Jake moved back to join them. "But I *did* see something. I know I did."

Ashley shrugged. "Something that doesn't register on a tricorder?" she asked skeptically.

"I suppose so." Jake knew it wasn't very convincing. And he had only caught a glimpse . . . Maybe there were mobile plants on this world that had furry edges that just *looked* like a hairy face? "Let's go on."

They reached the crash site only a few minutes later. The runabout lay as they'd left it, its bashed-in nose half buried in the ground. Ashley whistled in surprise and pointed at the grooves the crashing ship had sliced into the ground. "Will you look at that!" she exclaimed.

The huge furrow in the earth had already been half filled in by mosses and plants. They had either moved there or grown there already. Jake could almost see the edge of the green area slowly expanding to cover the bare earth. "These things don't waste much time, do they?" he asked.

"They've even started to grow over the runabout," Nog pointed out. It was true enough—several tall growths had already begun to twine about the shattered holes in the outside of the ship. In a few days the whole craft would disappear under the plant life.

"Then don't stand still too long," Ashley commented. "Otherwise they may start growing up your legs!" To Jake, she asked: "What does the power level read?"

Jake examined his tricorder. "Absolutely dead," he said, puzzled. "There's no sign of *anything* from the engines."

"Then it should be safe to go in," Ashley replied. She hurried across the clearing and made her way to the doorway. Then she pulled herself into the gap. As Jake hurried up behind her, he heard her cry out in shock.

Worried that something had happened to her, he pulled himself into the ship. As he stood up, he saw Ashley was safe and just staring about the craft. And then he saw why she'd been surprised.

The inside of the runabout had been stripped almost

bare. All of the panels had been opened up, and the spaces behind them where instruments should have been were empty. The control panel was gone. The supply cabinet had been opened, and the tools, the tricorders, and everything but a few packs had vanished. *Something* had taken the ship apart while they had been gone.

CHAPTER 8

What's happened?" asked Jake, amazed and appalled.

"Somebody beat us to it," Ashley said grimly. "Everything electronic seems to have been stripped from the ship. Including the subspace radio. And the tool kit!"

Nog and T'Ara joined them in the bare bones of the craft. "It's not fair!" cried Nog. "We were supposed to get the salvage!"

"It's worse than not fair," Ashley told him. "Without the radio, we can't call for help. We're well and truly stuck here now."

"Until someone gets worried enough to look for us," T'Ara suggested.

"More likely until the Cardassians find us," Jake replied bitterly. "We can't hide from them forever."

T'Ara paled a little at the thought. It was already clear enough that the Cardassians had been willing to kill

them all when they had opened fire on the runabout in space. It wasn't too likely that they'd be any more pleasant now that they were all on the planet together.

"You think that the Cardassians did this?" asked Jake.

"No way," Ashley answered. "According to the tricorders, they're still several kilometers away."

"According to the tricorders," Jake answered, "there's *nobody* around here but us. But *somebody* took all this stuff, and I don't believe it was a lot of light-fingered plants."

T'Ara held up her tricorder. "It still does not show anything," she said. "And it is not designed to run more complicated scans. We should not have needed anything more thorough than this."

Shaking his head in disgust, Jake crossed to the storage cabinets. He picked up one of the few bags remaining and opened it. There were several food packs inside it. "Well, at least whoever did this didn't steal all the food as well."

Ashley joined him. "Yeah," she agreed thoughtfully. "In fact, *all* the food packs are still here. Isn't it odd that they'd take all the equipment but leave the food?"

T'Ara raised an eyebrow. "If the Cardassians had been the thieves," she said, "they would have taken at least some of the food. They are able to eat it. This suggests that whoever took the electronic material cannot eat our food."

"Like the plants, you mean?" asked Jake. "But why would plants steal a radio?" He snapped his fingers. "Hey, what about that person I saw in the jungle?"

Ashley wrinkled her nose in disgust. "Nobody else saw anyone, Jake. And the tricorders didn't register anyone."

"They didn't show anyone *here,* either," Jake pointed out, gesturing around the stripped craft. "But somebody obviously was here. Maybe the same somebody the tricorder didn't see earlier?"

"If you *did* see someone," argued Ashley. Then she shook her head. "This planet is weird, and getting weirder every minute."

Nog growled. "There's no point in staying here," he objected. "Let's grab the food and head back to the cave before the food vanishes too. I'm hungry!"

Jake nodded. "We may as well," he agreed. But what were they going to tell Ms. O'Brien? Their last chance of calling for help was gone. While they had plenty of food now, they also had Cardassians out hunting for them— and some invisible force that had stripped the runabout. . . .

Ms. O'Brien couldn't explain what had happened, either. She was grateful that their food was intact, but the loss of the radio obviously hit her very badly. Jake knew she had to be thinking that this whole nightmare was her fault. The field trip here had been her idea, and she had convinced Jake's father that it was perfectly safe. But there had been no way she could have foreseen the problems that they had run into—especially not a Cardassian attack. Even granted that the Cardassians were not the nicest of people, they didn't usually react quite that badly.

So why had they attacked the runabout?

Their teacher stared helplessly at the bundled shape of Lieutenant Danvers. "He's in bad shape," she admitted. "I had hoped we could send for help. He's lost a lot of blood, and without some real medical care he's not likely to live more than a day or so. There *must* be something we can do!"

"If we could just figure out who took the equipment," Ashley suggested. "Then we could get it back, maybe."

"Oh, sure!" sneered Nog. He gestured at T'Ara. "She can't even find the culprits, let alone the missing stuff."

"It's not T'Ara's fault!" snapped Ashley. "She's doing her best!"

"Wait a minute," Jake said. "What about the equipment? Isn't it possible to scan for some of the elements in it? Like dilithium crystals or some of the rarer metals?"

T'Ara shook her head. "This world has too many metallic deposits," she replied. "And some of the plants have high concentrations of metal inside their stalks and leaves. It makes scanning for anything very difficult, unless there is an operating power source within it. That is the only way I can detect the Cardassian ship, and how you monitored the runabout until the power source stopped. The radio must have been stripped and its power source removed. It does not show up on my scans."

"So there's nothing we can do," said Jake with a sigh. He eyed the food pack he'd been given, along with a handful of the edible fruits and vegetables that Laren's gang had uncovered. "Well, I guess we might as well eat and then go to bed. There isn't much else to do." Then he remembered the vid-game his father had given him before they had left the station. "Unless anyone wants to play a game?" He pulled it from his backpack. "It's a baseball simulator."

"A game?" Nog shook his head. "I don't think I could stomach the idea of playing. We're in too much trouble. I just want to get totally depressed."

"Yeah." Jake shrugged. "There isn't much fun in playing at the minute, is there?" He replaced the game and then pulled the tab on his food pack. This started heating the contents, and in a few seconds he had a steaming pack of Bajoran bat-bird stew. Using a small stalk of one of the local plants as a spoon, he started to eat. Normally this was one of his favorite foods, but worry took the edge right off his appetite. His three friends sat with him, lost in their own thoughts. From the looks on their faces, they were just as miserable as Jake.

The Bajoran youngsters stayed huddled together around Laren. Bakis had finally stopped sniffling. Ms. O'Brien ate her own food with Molly. She stayed beside the unconscious pilot, watching him carefully as she ate.

Jake felt totally lost and hopeless. They were stuck here, and there didn't seem to be any way out of it. All that they could do was to try and hide from the Cardassians. At least with the tricorders they could tell where their enemies were. That was their only consolation right now.

After they had eaten, Jake stared out of the cave, across the jungle. The sun had set, and the last pale rays were dying out in the small portion of the sky he could see. There were sometimes faint glimmers from the stars visible, but it was mostly a mass of dark, twisted plant and tree shapes out there. Nobody said very much, as they were all too depressed to think of anything to say. Eventually Jake lay down using his backpack as a pillow and just drifted off to sleep.

It was still night when someone shook him awake. He sat up, and in the faint light he saw Ashley's worried face looking down at him. "Jake!" she whispered, her voice trembling. "The tricorders—they're all gone!"

CHAPTER 9

Gone?" echoed Jake, struggling to get his mind awake and functioning. "What do you mean *gone?*"

"Vanished," said T'Ara dryly. She was obviously hunched over next to Ashley. "I thought I heard a sound and awoke. I moved to pick up my tricorder, and it was not where I had left it. Then I wakened Ashley, and we searched for *any* of the tricorders. But none of them are to be found."

"Can't a guy get any sleep around here," grumbled Nog from nearby. "Go and bother somebody else, will you?"

"This is important," Jake told him.

"So's my sleep," Nog complained.

"How about your life?" asked Jake. He was keeping his voice low so as not to wake any of the others. "The tricorders are gone, and without them we can't tell where the Cardassians are."

Nog sat up suddenly. "That's horrible," he gasped, finally getting the picture.

Jake turned back to the girls. "You're certain they're all gone?" His own was definitely not where he'd placed it, on a rock beside his makeshift bed.

"All of them," Ashley insisted. "Now what do we do?"

Jake thought for a moment. "What did you hear that woke you?" he asked T'Ara. Vulcans had very good hearing, only partly due to the shape of their ears.

"I thought I had heard someone moving about," she said. "When I woke, though, I saw no one. I reached for my tricorder to scan the area, but it was not there."

"It's very odd," Jake said. "Somebody snuck into this cave just to steal our tricorders? It doesn't make any sense."

"It must have been the Cardassians," suggested Nog. "You know what thieves they are."

Jake shook his head. "No, I don't think so. If it was a Cardassian, why not capture us? Why just steal the tricorders? I think it was the same person or people who stripped the runabout. They're obviously after electronic stuff, and the tricorders were the only things left that—" He broke off as he remembered his vid-game. The pack was still on the ground where he'd been using it as a pillow. The game was still inside it, thankfully. But that was small consolation. "Well, they didn't get my game."

"They probably didn't want it," snapped Nog. "Baseball's boring."

T'Ara shook her head. "No; they probably couldn't get it, since Jake was using the pack as a pillow."

Jake was still thinking hard. "It must have been that little creature I saw in the jungle," he insisted. "I know that you all think I didn't see anything, but there is *something* out there stealing electronic equipment. I think I caught a glimpse of one of them, and it went back to the runabout to warn the others there we were coming."

"It is logical," agreed T'Ara. "Though unproven."

"Then let's prove it," said Jake firmly. He hated to do it, but he held up his vid-game. "We've got some bait here."

Ashley grinned. "You think the thief will be back for that?" she asked.

"It's stolen everything else," Jake answered. "I'll bet it can't resist this. All we have to do is catch the crook when he shows up for it."

"No problem," Nog said. "I'm an expert." Seeing Ashley's expression, he added: "At *catching* crooks, I mean." He gave a toothy grin. "I can use some of the creepers from the trees to make a real neat snare. Back in a minute." He scuttled out of the cave into the darkness beyond.

"You think this'll work?" asked Ashley. She sounded far from certain herself.

"It's got to," Jake said. "Without the tricorders, we've got no way of telling where the Cardassians are. They'll catch us for sure. But if we can capture one of the thieves, maybe we can get him, her, or it to talk—or maybe hold them hostage for the return of the stolen stuff."

T'Ara sighed. "I wish I knew why the tricorders did not register anything. It is like trying to catch a ghost."

Jake squirmed. "Don't say that," he begged. "I had enough problems with my last ghost; this character had better be flesh and blood."

"Flesh and blood would have shown up on my scanning," T'Ara told him.

There was a slight sound, and then Nog was back with them. "Got what I needed," he told them happily. "It'll only take me a few minutes to turn this stuff into a noose and a trigger. Why don't you figure out where you want the trap set?"

Jake held onto his vid-game as he walked slowly toward the cave entrance. Fairly close to it was a flat rock that could be seen from outside if their thief had good eyesight. Judging from the thief's activities so far, that was a pretty safe bet. "How about here?" Jake suggested.

"Good choice," agreed Ashley. She glanced about in the gloom. "T'Ara and I can camp over there, and you and Nog a bit further inside. Then we have to pretend to sleep, I guess."

"Right." Jake was reluctant to part with his game. It might vanish without a trace if Nog's trap didn't work. He was *almost* certain that Nog knew what he was doing with this trap of his, but there was a small doubt nibbling at his resolve. Still, he didn't really have any choice. This was their only chance to try and catch the thief and recover the essential equipment. And, he hoped, to unravel one of the mysteries of this planet.

"Here we go," said Nog quietly. He proceeded to lay out the noose beside the rock, covering it with a thin layer of soil. Then he set a thinner strand of fiber he'd taken from the creeper as a trip wire and used a couple of sticks to hold it all in place. Then he held out his hand to Jake. "Hand it over." With a deep sigh, Jake did so. Nog tied the end of the fiber to the game and set it carefully down on the rock. "All set."

"Well," Jake said reluctantly, "I guess we'd better pretend to go back to sleep, then, hadn't we?" Ashley and T'Ara nodded and moved off together. They settled down about ten feet away. Jake and Nog moved back deeper into the cave, closer to where Ms. O'Brien and the others were still sleeping soundly. "Do you think we should have told the teacher?" Jake asked Nog.

"Why?" the Ferengi boy replied. "She'd only have worried and wanted to take charge of the trap. We can wake her when we've caught the crook."

If we catch him, thought Jake, but he didn't say it aloud. There was so much that could go wrong. As he settled down to pretend to sleep, all the possible problems went through his mind. What if their mysterious thief had watched them set the trap? Then he wouldn't come near it. Or what if he was a ghostlike being, as T'Ara had suggested? He might be able to walk through the trap without setting it off. Then again, if the thief wasn't real, how could he steal real stuff? But Jake knew there were beings that were real but not flesh and blood.

The people that made the Wormhole, for example—they were like energy that could solidify into real bodies, but didn't need to. Maybe the alien thief was like one of them?

At least he didn't have to worry about falling asleep while he waited to see if the thief came back. He was so worried, there was no way he'd get any more sleep tonight. Would the thief bother coming back for just one stupid vid-game? Maybe the bait wasn't worth the risk. Or maybe Jake really *had* just imagined that creature in the woods. But if it wasn't that hairy thing he'd seen, then what had stripped the runabout and stolen the tricorders?

At least one thing had become a little clearer. It was obvious now why the Cardassians hadn't been able to track their little party—whoever their thief was must have already taken the Cardassians' tricorders and scanners. It certainly seemed as if the thief or thieves were really active—and very, very greedy.

In which case, they shouldn't be able to resist the bait.

Time passed. Jake had his eyes open just a slit and lay facing the rock. He could see a faint gleam from the metal box of the vid-game as he watched. He could hear grunting sounds from Nog behind him, but he didn't know if Nog had fallen asleep or was just pretending to have fallen asleep. He didn't dare move to try and find out. It would be just like Nog to nod off, though, right when he was most needed. In fact—

Jake almost jumped. There was the faint flicker of something moving in the opening to the cave. From this angle he couldn't make out anything more than that. But he hadn't been imagining it. A few seconds later he caught another flicker of motion out of the corner of his eye.

The thief had come back—but would the bait be taken?

Hardly daring to breathe, Jake waited. It seemed like hours before there was another movement. This time there was absolutely no mistaking it. A little light from the night sky was entering the cave, and a shadowy shape passed behind this, heading directly for the rock. Jake couldn't make much out, except that the figure was small and squat. Definitely no Cardassian, then, because they were all tall and skinny. The little shape was right beside the rock where the vid-game sat. There was another swift movement—

—and a howl of shock and terror as Nog's trap sprang. The shadowy figure was jerked from its feet as the noose tightened about its foot.

Jake leaped to his feet and dashed toward the rock. Nog, Ashley, and T'Ara followed him. In the back of the cave, Ms. O'Brien, Laren and the rest were startled awake by the noise. Before the terrified thief could struggle out of the noose about its ankle, Jake had a firm grip on a hairy arm. Then he stared in shock at the strangest creature he had ever seen in his life.

CHAPTER 10

Their captive was quivering in fear. Jake had a firm grip on one of the little man's arms, and Ashley had her own grip on the other. The small person was only about one meter tall, and very stocky. Jake's earlier glimpse in the jungle had been correct—the thief was covered in dark hair. It looked like a troll, with two bright eyes, slits for nostrils that were quivering with fear, and a small mouth with tiny teeth. It was dressed in a kind of leather jacket and pants, but its large, hairy feet were quite bare.

None of this made the creature that bizarre. Stranger aliens passed through Deep Space Nine all the time. What was really weird about this person was that parts of the skin and flesh were missing and had been replaced with electronic components or circuits. Several of these glowed, pulsed, or shifted shapes. It was as if their captive was half computer. Part of one arm was mechanical, and half of its neck. Behind the left ear was a clear patch of shiny metal, with a socket visible. Two of the creature's stubby fingers were metallic, and one ended in a probe.

"What *are* you?" asked T'Ara in fascination.

"What's going on?" called Ms. O'Brien.

"We've caught the little thief," Nog replied, looking very pleased with himself. "And boy, is he ugly!"

"Talk you should," their captive grunted. "Pretty you aren't." He still looked scared, but at the same time he was obviously striving to be as brave as possible.

"What's your name?" Jake asked the little being.

"Hurt me you won't?" asked the creature anxiously.

"No, we won't," promised Jake. "We just want the things you stole returned."

Their captive's face fell. "Possible is not," he said sadly. He looked over their shoulders as Ms. O'Brien appeared, still clutching a sleepy Molly. The young girl brightened up when she saw the hairy little figure.

"Cute," she said, smiling.

"What are you?" asked the teacher, staring in amazement at the little man.

The thief was staring back at Molly, clearly puzzled and pleased to see the child. "Baby is yours?" he asked the teacher.

"Baby is mine," agreed Ms. O'Brien, clearly puzzled by this remark.

"Baby I have too," he replied proudly.

"That's nice," said Jake sarcastically. "Our tricorders and other stuff you have, too." The little being's odd way of talking was getting infectious. "And we've gotta have them back."

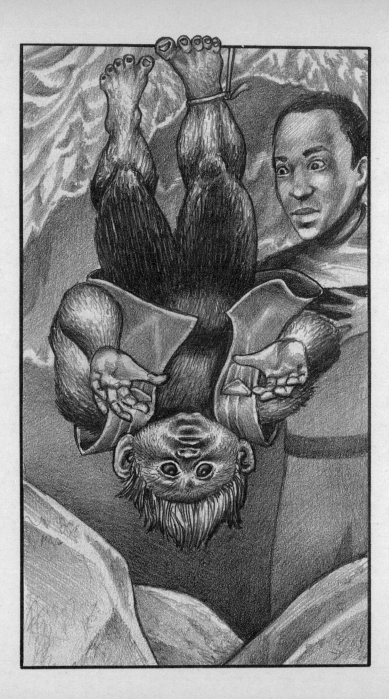

"Possible is not," the little person repeated. "Have it we must."

Ms. O'Brien settled down beside them, holding Molly firmly. "Can you explain what is happening here?" she asked the thief.

The little man looked troubled. "Trust you I can?" he asked. "Tell the Cardassians you won't?"

"Trust *us?*" asked Nog in disgust. "Hey, you're the thief around here."

"And we're certainly not talking to the Cardassians," added Laren firmly. "They tried to kill us. And they invaded my planet."

"Kill us too they tried," their captive said.

"There's more of you?" asked Ms. O'Brien.

The little man hesitated a moment and then nodded. "In hiding we are. Trofars we are." He tried to tap his chest, but Jake didn't let go of his arm. "Lek I am."

"Well, Lek," said the teacher, "I think you should try and explain what's going on, don't you?"

Lek nodded. "Explain I will. Release me you will?" He looked up at Jake and Ashley.

"You won't try and run away?" asked Jake. He couldn't help but like the little creature. The Trofar was obviously calming down a bit now that he knew he wasn't going to be immediately hurt, but he still looked a little scared.

"My word I give," Lek replied. "Stay I will. Explain I will."

Jake looked to the teacher for guidance, and she gave him a quick nod. Jake let go of the Trofar's arm, and

Ashley did the same. The little person gave them a grin, then settled down on the rock so he could look at them as he talked.

"Trofar I am," he explained. "A planet far, far away our home is. By the Cardassians taken we were. Good at hiding we are, but with instruments captured us they did." His face twisted from bad memories. "Hurt us they did. Changed us they did." He tapped one of his implants with his probe finger. "Machines to us they added."

"That's horrible," muttered Ashley. "But why did they do that?"

"Good at hiding we were," Lek told them. "But with the implants better at hiding we are. Before the implants, tricorders and sensors find us they could. Now find us they can't. Invisible we are."

"Invisible you're not," scoffed Nog. "We can see you."

"See me you can," agreed Lek. "See us sensors can't. Stop us deflectors can't. Hold us out force barriers can't. Between them all we slip."

Ms. O'Brien shook her head in wonder. "You mean they've added all kinds of electronic implants that make you invisible to sensors? And that you can get through force fields?"

"Correct absolutely you are," Lek agreed. "Spies and saboteurs of us the Cardassians want. Steal things, blow things up they demand."

Jake was starting to understand now. The Cardassians had taken the Trofars, who were a shy people very skilled at hiding. Then by adding some electronics to them, they had made the little people able to hide from sensors as well. People like that could slip in anywhere and be the perfect secret agents! That was why their tricorders hadn't been able to pick up the Trofars. They *couldn't*.

"Wow!" he exclaimed. "So what did you do?"

"Refused we did," Lek answered. "Peaceful we are. Spies we are not. Saboteurs and killers we are not. Furious the Cardassians are."

"I'll bet," said Ms. O'Brien. "They wouldn't like you refusing to do what they told you."

"Like it definitely they didn't," agreed Lek sadly. "Killed some of us they did. Ultimatum they gave us then. Spies and killers we become or dead we become." He shook his head. "Not happy we were." Then he gave another grin. "But smart we are. Oh, yes, *very* smart we are. And invisible to sensors we are. Out of Cardassian cells we escaped. Through their buildings we ran." He tapped his chest proudly. "Leader I am. Plan I had. Their spaceport close by lay. A ship there we found. Onto it we crept. *Whoosh!* Into space we escaped. Great pilot I am." His face twitched. "But after us they came. Fired on us they did. Crashed in the jungle here our ship did. After us the Cardassians came. In hiding we are. In trouble we are."

"I can just imagine you are," the teacher told him.

"Equipment we need," Lek explained. "The Cardassian ship we sneak aboard. Their equipment, some of it we take. Enough it is not. Then another ship it comes. Late, late the Cardassians know this. Scared they are Federation will find us. Scared they are against the

Cardassians we will turn. Shoot down your ship they must. *Whoosh!* Offward they take. Down you come. After you the Cardassians hunt. Our chance this is. Your ship with equipment is full."

"So you stripped everything you could from the runabout?" asked T'Ara.

"Correct you are," Lek admitted. "Have it we must."

"Greedy you are," growled Nog. "Then you followed us here and stole the tricorders, too?"

Lek nodded. "Have them we must," he insisted. He looked longingly at the vid-game. "This too is needed."

"Needed for what?" asked Ms. O'Brien. "Why do you need all of this electronic equipment? And why can't you give it back?"

Lek stared at her in astonishment. "Understand you don't?" He pointed to Molly. "Baby you have."

"And you're not having *her,*" said the teacher firmly.

"Want her I don't," Lek said. "Baby I have." He stared at them all. "Babies we all have."

"Oh!" T'Ara's eyes opened wide as she finally understood what he was saying. "You mean *now!*" She looked at Ms. O'Brien. "Lek means that the Trofars are having babies right here and now."

"Correct you are!" agreed Lek happily. "Understand you do. Babies we have—now!" He tapped the vid-game. "Changed by the Cardassians we are. Genetically altered we are. Part electronic *we* are. New babies are not. Without many parts, die the babies will. Need them we do."

Jake finally understood what the little creature meant.

The Cardassians had altered the Trofars, making them utterly dependent on their electronic implants. It was a way of trying to control their slaves. The babies would be born, and without immediate implants the babies would die. The Trofars had been forced to steal everything they could to make the implants their babies needed. He couldn't blame Lek and his friends for what they had done. But by stealing the equipment, the Trofars might have doomed them all to be killed by the Cardassians.

CHAPTER 11

Terrific," said Ashley with a deep sigh. "We caught our thief, but we don't get anything back except a headache."

Jake could understand his friend's disappointment. He, too, had been counting on their plan to get them off this planet before the Cardassians could catch them. Now all it seemed to have netted them was a new friend who was even more keen to hide from their hunters. "So what do we do now?" he asked.

Lek looked at them all. "Help us you will?" he asked.

"How can we help you?" asked Jake reasonably. "We need help ourselves."

Lek tapped Ms. O'Brien on the arm. "Mother you are. Help us you can. Not used to children we are. First of the new Trofars these are. Expectant most of our females are."

The teacher caught on. "Your women need help with the babies?" she asked. Lek nodded. Ms. O'Brien bit at her lip in indecision. "I can't leave my students," she

86

finally said. Jake knew that she wanted to help the Trofars, too.

"Bring them along you can," Lek told her happily. "Nice cave we have. Hold us all it will. Help us you can."

The teacher looked over at Lieutenant Danvers. "And we have an injured man."

"Bring him we must," Lek said. "Some medicines we have."

Ms. O'Brien sighed. "In that case, one cave is as good as another. And if we stick together, we can watch out for the Cardassians better, I suppose." She looked out of the cave. "It's starting to get light," she said. "And I think everyone's well and truly awake." She raised her voice to reach all of the students. The Bajorans were staring in fascination at the little Trofar, still seated on the rock. "All right, everybody. Gather up the supplies. We're going to be moving to another cave." With the arm that wasn't holding Molly, she gestured to the little alien. "This is Lek. He and his people need our help and friendship. He'll be leading the way. Everyone must stay very quiet so we don't attract the Cardassians."

Lek and Nog conferred for a moment, then went off together into the jungle. They returned in a few minutes with long sticks, several large leaves, and various creepers. Together the Trofar and the Ferengi quickly assembled a stretcher. Ms. O'Brien helped them to move the still-sleeping pilot onto it. Jake immediately took the front. To his surprise, Laren insisted on taking the other end.

With Lek leading the way, they set off in the early

morning half-light. It was eerie walking through the thick jungle as the sun started to rise. Everything was soaked in a green light, and all about them the plants were waking to the sun. Huge flowers that had curled up for the night awoke and spread out to catch the rising rays. In the distance several Screaming Mimis could be heard, howling as they rolled through the shrubs. They had to skirt around several of the Tingle Tanglers that were waiting for unwary prey, but nothing else seemed to be very interested in them. The day was already warm, and the walk was like a stroll in a park. It was difficult to remember sometimes that there were Cardassians out there hunting for everyone in this little group. It seemed so pleasant and peaceful here.

The walk wasn't a long one. Within fifteen minutes they arrived at another cave entrance. Lek grinned and beckoned them all on. Another Trofar suddenly stepped from the bushes ahead of them. He must have been watching the group approach, but Jake hadn't seen any sign of him until he stepped out of the jungle. He was almost identical to Lek, but he had a darker green jacket than Lek's almost lime-colored one.

"Friends these are," Lek told his companion, who was staring in astonishment at the students. "Help they will. Hate the Cardassians, too, they do."

The Trofar sentry nodded solemnly. "Welcome then they are." He gave everyone a smile, and then disappeared once more into the foliage. In a second, there was again no sign of him.

Lek gave Jake an encouraging nod. "Guard he is. If the

Cardassians come, warn us he will." He led the way into the cave.

It was very like the one that they had recently left, except it seemed deeper and higher. At intervals about the cave light-sticks had been placed to shed their rays over the huddled groups. Jake gasped, staring at the Trofars there. There were about twenty of them, most of them female. Of those, almost all had swollen bellies, showing they were expecting babies any time. One Trofar female had already given birth, and she clutched a tiny, furry bundle protectively to her chest. Jake could see the glimmer of electronic parts on all the Trofars, and even on this newborn infant.

Scattered about the cave were the remnants of the stolen goods. All of the larger equipment had been torn apart and used to build smaller implants. The bodies from the tricorders had been tossed aside like broken eggshells. Other panels had been gutted and cast aside. Several of the Trofars—male and female—were still working on stripping electronic materials and building the necessary implants for the impending births.

Everything stopped as the small party entered the cave. Bright, scared eyes stared at the newcomers. Lek threw up his hands. "Friends these are," he declared loudly. "Help us they will." He gestured toward Ms. O'Brien. "Mother she too is."

"The poor things," said Ms. O'Brien softly, looking about. "I'd better get to work. Jake, you and Laren set Lieutenant Danvers down over there by those rocks. I can keep an eye on everybody all together that way. The

rest of you settle down but try to stay out of the way." She hurried across to the main group of females and started to examine them as best she could.

As soon as Jake had made the pilot as comfortable as he could, he rejoined his friends. Ashley and T'Ara were examining what was left of the stolen equipment, but even Jake could see it was hopeless even to think about rebuilding a subspace transmitter. "There's no way to get a message out, then?" he asked.

"Not with this stuff," Ashley answered. She sounded very depressed. "These Trofars are just too good at scavenging. Even better than Nog."

"Nobody's better than me," Nog said, sniffing.

"Then *you* figure out how to get a distress call out," snapped Ashley.

"All right," agreed Nog. He turned to Lek. "Do the Cardassians still have a subspace radio on board?"

Ashley gave an incredulous laugh. "You think you can just knock on their door and ask to use the phone?" she asked.

"I was actually thinking that we could *scavenge* it," Nog replied with dignity.

"Too late you are," Lek informed him. "Scavenged already it is."

Nog sighed. "Why did I suspect you were gonna say that?"

"Wait a minute," Jake said. An idea was starting to form in his mind. "I think you're on to something here. We don't have any equipment left, but the Cardassians do."

Lek shook his head. "Taken it all is. Tricorders, radio, everything we took."

"Not *everything*," Jake replied with a grin. "They still have a working spaceship."

His friends all stared at him as if he were crazy. T'Ara's eyebrows rose so high they almost merged with her bangs. "Are you suggesting . . . ?"

"Yeah." Jake chuckled. "Let's scavenge their entire ship!"

CHAPTER 12

"Hit your head have you?" asked Lek, his eyes wide. "Dreaming perhaps are you?"

"I'm not crazy and I'm not dreaming," Jake replied. "Look, it's our only chance to get out of here, isn't it?"

"You *are* crazy," Ashley told him. "We can't fight six armed Cardassians!"

"We don't have to," Jake answered. "Four of them are out looking for us. There are only two of them left with their ship. And they won't be expecting trouble. They're probably just there to make sure that the Trofars don't steal anything else."

"True that is," agreed Lek cheerfully.

"Yeah," Nog said admiringly. "Anything that's not nailed down they steal."

"Nailed down things also we steal," Lek said proudly. "Even nails we steal." Then he frowned. "Spaceships steal we don't."

"Yes, you do," T'Ara broke in. "You told us that you stole the one you escaped from the Cardassians in."

Lek cocked his head to one side. "True that is. Spaceships steal we do."

"Right," said Jake. "This spaceship steal we will. All we have to do is deal with the two Cardassians still there."

"Oh, yeah, right," said Ashley. "Two Cardassians? No problem. Jake, we don't even have any weapons!"

Nog grinned. "Sure we do."

Ashley glared at him. "What? You have a peashooter hidden in your ear?"

Nog shook his head. "Your trouble is that you never learned to scavenge. Weapons are whatever you can make or find."

T'Ara raised an eyebrow. "We may be able to make bows and arrows. Or spears."

Ashley shook her head. "First of all, T'Ara, *making* them doesn't mean we can use them. Have you ever tried shooting a bow and arrow? And against a phaser? And second, we'd have to wound or kill with them, and I don't think I could do that, even to a Cardassian."

"Killing we do not," agreed Lek.

"I wasn't thinking of that kind of weapon," Nog said. "I was thinking of the plants." Seeing their blank expressions, he sighed. "Look, the plant life around here is adaptable, right? I already made a Trofar trap. I'll bet we could make a Cardassian catcher just as easily."

Jake nodded enthusiastically. "That's the idea! I'll bet

94

we can come up with a surefire way to get that Cardassian ship."

"That is possible," agreed T'Ara cautiously. "But what do we do with it if we get it? Lieutenant Danvers is our only pilot, and he is not in a fit state to walk, let alone fly a shuttle."

Lek growled and slapped his chest. "Pilot I am!" he exclaimed. "Fly anything I can. *Whoosh!* Off this planet we go."

Ashley looked at her friends and then shrugged. "Well, maybe it's *possible,*" she agreed reluctantly. "But do you think Ms. O'Brien will agree to this? She'll go ballistic!"

"Only if we tell her," Jake said reluctantly. He didn't like the thought of keeping this from their teacher, but he knew Ms. O'Brien *would* go ballistic and forbid them even to try. "I'm pretty sure Laren will cover for us and look after her friends. And Ms. O'Brien is going to be kept pretty busy with the babies and all. We've gotta try this. Otherwise the Cardassians are bound to catch us all, aren't they? That means Lek and his people will be forced to become spies for the Cardassians or be killed." He frowned. "And now that we know about the Trofars, the Cardassians aren't gonna let us go free, are they?"

"That would not be logical," T'Ara agreed. "They are much more likely to kill us all."

"Anyway," argued Nog, "we're gonna be with an adult or two, right?" He grinned at Lek. "You guys are adults, aren't you?"

"Very very adult I am," Lek replied.

"So," asked Jake, "do you think you and maybe another of your friends might be able to help us scavenge the Cardassian ship?"

Lek grinned happily. "Very very pleasurable it will be. Tad help us he will. Together the Cardassians beat we will."

Jake nodded. "Let's hope you're right."

Tad was the Trofar who was on duty outside the cave. Another of the Trofar males relieved him. While Ms. O'Brien was checking the mothers-to-be, Jake took a look at Lieutenant Danvers. The pilot was breathing shallowly now, and his leg was swollen. He was pale and obviously in very bad shape. Without medical help Jake was certain the pilot would die. This strengthened his resolve to go through with their planned raid on the Cardassians. He spoke to Laren, telling her of their plan.

"I want to come along," she said firmly. "I'll be more help than anyone."

"And who'd look after Bakis and the others?" Jake asked her. "He's almost in tears again. You're the only one who can keep their spirits up. And to stop Ms. O'Brien from finding out we've gone."

Laren sighed. "I never get to have any fun. But I guess you're right." She grinned. "I'll stay—but the next war you start, I want in on, right?"

"Promise," agreed Jake.

With Ms. O'Brien distracted, Jake, Nog, Ashley, T'Ara, Lek, and Tad managed to sneak out of the cave without being observed. Quickly they headed back through the jungle toward the landing site of the Cardassian ship. Tad went on ahead to scout, so that he could warn them all if the searching Cardassians came close.

They traveled quietly, just in case, and stopped several times on the way to collect specimens of various plants that they would be needing for their attack. Once they had to wade across a small stream that was just as peculiar as the rest of the planet. There were no fish, of course, but there were small lily pad-like plants that moved about the water, using large vertical leaves like sails, and trailing tendrils in the water to grasp and feast from other plants.

Tad had them make one small detour to avoid the only Cardassian that came anywhere near them. Thanks to his warning, they didn't even see the hunters. And at the end of three hours of traveling, Tad stopped them once again.

"Ahead the ship is," he reported softly. "On duty outside one guard is."

Jake nodded. "Then the second one must be inside the ship. Anything else?"

"Forcefield about the doorway is," Tad said.

"Us it will not stop," Lek pointed out. "You it will stop. Cardassian on duty with gun all of us will stop."

"Right," agreed Jake. "So we get only one try at this. Is everybody ready?" He glanced at them each in turn and received nods. Swallowing hard to try and force down his own worries and attack of nerves, he said: "Okay— time to get into positions. Then the raid begins!"

CHAPTER 13

If the attack didn't work, Jake knew that the Cardassians wouldn't hesitate to shoot. From his hiding place he could see the ship and the guard on duty. They were about twelve meters away in a small clearing. The ship was an antique patrol craft, probably a veteran of the Cardassian-Bajoran Wars, but it looked in workable shape. The guard was tall, almost impossibly thin and gray, with the snakelike head of all the Cardassians. He held a disrupter rifle in his hands, but it was pointed at the ground. He was on guard, but obviously not expecting trouble right now.

Well, he was going to get trouble. Jake held the Tingle Tangler pod very carefully in his hand. When he heard the signal, he'd get a chance to put all his baseball practice into use.

Nog had to be in position by now, surely. . . . How much longer was Jake going to have to sit here, sweating and nervous, waiting for the signal?

Then he heard it. There was a crashing sound in the undergrowth north of the ship. The guard suddenly whipped around, his rifle coming up when a horrible howling and screaming broke out. The Screaming Mimi that Nog had released ran across the clearing, yelling its nonexistent head off. The guard, obviously used to such noises, visibly relaxed and lowered his rifle. His back was now turned to Jake.

Jake stood up silently, flexed his arm, and then pitched. Like a baseball, the Tingle Tangle pod zipped through the air. A perfect throw! It slammed right into the unprepared Cardassian's back and cracked open.

In a flurry of motion, the Tingle Tangler's tentacles shot out, enveloping the startled guard. There was a brief flash of light as the electrical charge in the pod zapped through the Cardassian. With a startled grunt, the guard collapsed, stunned.

Lek and Tad shot out of the jungle, lassos made from creepers in their hands. Before the stunned Cardassian could react, they had him trussed up on the ground, with a sticky leaf plastered over his mouth to prevent him from sounding an alarm.

Ashley and T'Ara slipped out of hiding and ran to join them. Jake and Nog moved carefully over to keep an eye on the guard while the two Trofars did their job. The hatch into the Cardassian ship was open, but there was the faint shimmering of a security field in the gap. Lek grinned and winked, then simply slipped sideways through the screen. His electronic implants glowed and flickered as they diverted the field that was supposed to keep anyone out. Jake could see why the Cardassians were desperate to get the Trofars back and working for them. Nowhere was safe from the little creatures!

Ashley was poised to follow him, waiting only for the second that Lek switched off the field inside. She and T'Ara also held their plant weapons ready to use. A moment after Lek had entered the craft, the barrier collapsed. The two girls ran inside, with Jake, Nog, and Tad hot on their heels.

The ship was a little musty inside, and the lighting was low-level. Jake blinked to get used to it, then dashed after his friends for the control cabin. By the time he arrived, the final Cardassian was already enveloped in two Tingle Tanglers. As he collapsed, the Trofars whipped their creeper lariats about him and firmly tied him up. Between them, they then hoisted him over their heads and ran back to the hatch. With great glee, they tossed him outside and then sealed the hatch behind them.

The two Trofars headed back to the cabin dancing and clapping with glee. "Very very good we are!" Lek crowed. "Very very smart and very very brave!" He gave a huge grin to Jake and his friends. "Brilliant and brave also you all are!"

Ashley had slipped into the co-pilot's seat and was examining the board. "Well, it looks as if the ship's in operating condition," she announced. She tapped one of the panels where there was a conspicuous hole. "The Trofars apparently stole only the sensors and radio before the Cardassians sealed the ship."

"Stole them we did," agreed Lek, dropping into the pilot's chair. "Need them for flying we don't."

Nog stared at the controls, all labeled in the Cardassian language. "You can read that scrawl?" he asked Ashley in amazement.

"Nah," she admitted, tapping the controls. "But the systems in this thing are just like the ones back on the station. And I know them all backward, so this should be a breeze. Powering up the engines," she informed Lek. "How's it look there?"

"Very very wonderful it looks," the Trofar answered. "Upward and onward we go!" With a howl of pleasure he slapped home the last few levers, then grabbed the steering column.

Jake almost fell over as the Cardassian ship suddenly rose from the ground. He grabbed for a handhold and clung to it for dear life. Lek had obviously been telling the truth when he claimed he could fly the ship, but it was obvious that he could have used a few more lessons. The craft buckled and shivered as it soared.

"We did it!" Jake yelled happily. He grinned at his friends. Even T'Ara was so pleased that she smiled back before remembering she was a Vulcan and wasn't supposed to show happiness.

The trip back to the cave took less than three minutes. Jake wondered what the four Cardassian searchers must be thinking when they saw their ship pass overhead. It probably wouldn't occur to them for a while yet that they had been stranded. He wished he could see their faces when that did dawn on them, though!

Jake saw the mountain appear above the trees, and then Lek was piloting in for a bumpy but safe landing. The students and the Trofars in hiding had to be certain that the Cardassians had somehow found them, and Jake could imagine the panic that must be spreading right now. As soon as the ship was down, he, Nog, and Tad ran to the hatch and slapped the controls to open it. Then they rushed down.

"It's okay!" Jake yelled at the top of his lungs. "It's only us! We captured the Cardassian ship!"

Two Trofars immediately appeared out of the trees, staring at the three happy arrivals in astonishment. "Amazed I am!" one of them said. "Incredible it is!"

"You can say that again," Nog agreed. "Aren't we just astonishing?"

By the time Jake and Nog reached the cave, almost all

the Trofar males had joined them. Ms. O'Brien was in the opening, staring in amazement at them—and then beyond them to the waiting ship.

"What have you done?" she gasped.

"We captured the Cardassian ship," Jake said proudly. "Now we can get off the planet."

The teacher shook her head in astonishment. "I can hardly believe it," she said. Then she fixed her eyes on him. "You're going to have to explain this when we get back to Deep Space Nine," she said. "And then your father and I will probably draw straws to see which one of us gets to skin you alive."

Jake suddenly realized that he and his friends might be heroes right now . . . but that could just change once they returned home. They *had* taken an awful risk, but what other choice did they really have? On the other hand, would his father see it quite that way?

"Pretty neat," Laren told them approvingly. "I just wish I could have helped more."

Ms. O'Brien wasted no time. She promptly organized everyone to get the pregnant Trofars aboard the ship. Jake and Laren carried the stretcher aboard. Lieutenant Danvers was still unconscious, but at least it wouldn't be long before he was able to get real medical help back on the station.

Bakis started sniffing again. "It smells funny in there," he complained.

"Then stop breathing," Laren suggested unsympathetically. "We're going home."

Jake wished he knew what was going to happen to him when he got back. . . .

Jake's father finished hearing the story in silence, and then rose slowly to his feet. Jake gave Nog, Ashley, and T'Ara nervous glances, wondering if they were going to be in trouble. Instead of talking to them, however, Commander Sisko turned to Lek.

"And how are your people now?" he asked. "I understand that Dr. Bashir has been helping out with the births."

"Good they are," the Trofar replied. "Fascinated the doctor is. Papers he speaks of writing. Healthy and strong the babies are. Happy and rested the mothers are."

"I'm very pleased to hear it," the commander replied. "What are your plans now? Do you want to go back to your original world again?"

"Sad to say that this possible is not," Lek replied, looking downcast. "No longer like other Trofars we are. Welcome not we would be. Outcasts we are."

"That's a shame." Jake's father tapped his notepad. "So you're looking for a new home, then? Starfleet would be more than happy to help out there."

Lek wrinkled his nose as he concentrated. "Spies and saboteurs against the Cardassians you want us to be?" he asked warily.

"No. We don't do that sort of thing in the Federation. Happy is all we want you to be." He laid a hand on Lek's small shoulder. "You and your people can choose what you wish to do. Nobody in the Federation will force you to do anything you don't like."

"Good that is," said Lek happily. "New home we will find."

"Then I think that wraps up matters," said Commander Sisko. "Dr. Bashir informs me that he is confident that we could reverse your dependence on the implants if that is what you wish. It's your decision to make."

"Think about it we will," Lek agreed.

"Good. And Dr. Bashir also tells me that Lieutenant Danvers' life was saved by getting him back here, and he's well on the way to recovery now. That's almost all, I think."

"But what about the Cardassians?" exclaimed Ashley. "They hurt the Trofars, and they shot down our runabout. Shouldn't they be punished?"

Jake's father smiled tightly. "I'm sure they *are* being punished—by their own people. For letting the Trofars escape."

"Speak of the devil," said Major Kira from the other side of the room. "There's an incoming message from Gul Dukat."

Commander Sisko raised an eyebrow. "Put it through."

The small viewer in front of him lit up, showing the gray face of the Cardassian who had once commanded Deep Space Nine. "Commander Sisko, I hear that some

of your people had an unfortunate run-in with some criminals of my people."

"Criminals?" asked Jake's father evenly. "I was under the impression that they were Cardassian military personnel."

Gul Dukat managed to look astonished at the thought. "What an idea! No, indeed—they were a small group of vicious crooks who were conducting illegal scientific experiments."

"I see," said the commander. "Nothing to do with the Cardassian military at all?"

"Absolutely not." Gul Dukat smiled. "But my men have arrested them all, and I assure you that they will be most appropriately punished."

"I'm relieved to hear that," Commander Sisko said. "And I take it that you have no desire to see the Trofars again?"

Gul Dukat said, "I've never seen a Trofar at all. How could I wish to see one again? As a gesture of goodwill, I've had your damaged runabout recovered and it will be returned to you very shortly. We will, naturally, pay the cost of all repairs." He spread his hands. "Once more, my sincerest apologies for what has occurred." The screen went dead.

"Liar that one is," Lek snapped. "Very very lying he is."

"I'm sure he is," agreed Jake's father. "But there's no way we can prove it right now. And while he and his people did some terrible things to you, you're free now.

You even have a starship of your own and lots of healthy children to look after. And speaking of children . . ." He stared at Jake. Jake's face went hot. "The four of you were very brave. And very foolish, too. However, under the circumstances, I feel that you didn't really have any option but to act as you did." He almost smiled. "You did well. But if you try anything like that ever again, I shall be very tempted to ground you all until you're a hundred. Dismissed." He turned his back on them.

Jake didn't wait. He led the others out of the room and sighed with relief as the door closed behind them. "We got off light," he muttered.

Nog grimaced. "I think we should have been given medals for what we did."

"I'm just glad we weren't punished," Ashley admitted.

"Nog!" They all heard Quark's voice as he approached them. "I heard that you were back. I was so worried!"

Nog looked surprised and pleased. "About me?" he asked.

"You? No, about the plant samples." Quark stopped in his tracks and stared at him in concern. "You did remember to bring some back, didn't you?"

"Yeah." Nog sighed and handed over his backpack. "They're in here."

"I can't wait to see them," Quark gloated. "I'm gonna be rich from this!" Snatching the pack, he hurried off, fumbling with the releases.

"We're gonna be rich!" yelled Nog after him. Then he

looked at his friends. "He's gonna try and cheat me," he said. "I just know he is."

T'Ara inclined her head gravely. "It is logical that he will try."

Jake grinned. "Well, we're all okay, anyway, and—" He broke off as he heard a horrible scream from around the corridor corner.

"That's Uncle Quark!" exclaimed Nog. "What do you think happened?" He started to move forward, but Jake grabbed his arm.

"I think he just opened one of the Tingle Tangler specimens you brought back," he said. "This may not be the best time to talk to him about a share of the profits."

Nog gulped and nodded. "I think it's more like time to find somewhere to hide again!" He ran off down the corridor in the opposite direction as fast as he could.

Ashley smiled. "Well, I guess things are back to normal around here."

"I guess they are," agreed Jake. It felt good to be back on the station again. "I guess they are."

About the Author

JOHN PEEL was born in Nottingham, England—home of Robin Hood. He moved to the U.S. in 1981 to get married and now lives on Long Island with his wife, Nan, and their wire-haired fox terrier, Dashiell. He has written more than fifty books, including novels based on the top British science fiction TV series, *Doctor Who,* and the top American science fiction TV series, *Star Trek.* His novel, *Star Trek: The Next Generation: Here There Be Dragons,* is available from Pocket Books. He has also written several supernatural thrillers for young adults that are published by Archway Paperbacks— *Talons, Shattered, Poison,* and *Maniac.* His first story about Jake and Nog, *Star Trek: Deep Space Nine: Prisoners of Peace,* is available from Minstrel Books.

About the Illustrator

TODD CAMERON HAMILTON is a self-taught artist who has resided all his life in Chicago, Illinois. He has been a professional illustrator for the past ten years, specializing in fantasy, science fiction, and horror. Todd is the current president of the Association of Science Fiction and Fantasy Artists. His original works grace many private and corporate collections. He has co-authored two novels and several short stories. When not drawing, painting, or writing, his interests include metalsmithing, puppetry, and teaching.

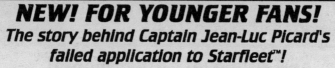